Narwhal

Thank you Lloyd for today

NARWHAL

Margaret Gill

Margaret

iUniverse, Inc.

New York Lincoln Shanghai

Narwhal

iUniverse books may be ordered through booksellers or by contacting:

iUniverse
2021 Pine Lake Road, Suite 100
Lincoln, NE 68512
www.iuniverse.com
1-800-Authors (1-800-288-4677)

Because of the dynamic nature of the Internet, any Web addresses
or links contained in this book may have changed
since publication and may no longer be valid.

This is a work of fiction. All of the characters, names, incidents, organizations,
and dialogue in this novel are either the products of the author's imagination
or are used fictitiously.

ISBN: 978-0-595-48177-4 (pbk)
ISBN: 978-0-595-60274-2 (ebk)

Printed in the United States of America

For the children of Year 6 (2007) Walgrave Primary School, whose enthusiasm for the story was so refreshing and inspiring.

A calm sea now, a gentle isle and fair
Named Agnes, Lamb of God, saintly, pure.
Smooth are the sunlit backs of docile cows.
Heady the tang of moorland ling and salt seaweed.

Beyond the cricket pitch
A preening gull presides over
The newly towered church and quiet bay,
Basking in virgin air, loving the light,
Lulled by an unctuous, silky sea.

One face holy, quiet; the other secret, cruel, deep
In places where smooth grass gives way
To darkened, slimy, salt edged pools
Shadowed by wind tortured stone,
Where lie bleached skulls, jetsam
Of a violent sea.

Here the Western rocks glint greedily
Like dragon's teeth ringing the Bishop,
Waiting to slash and maul, when the sun's fire
Drops down to temper those steel needles
That will rend bowsprit, shrouds and men
Lured by Agnes, now the treacherous siren maid.

Author's Note

Scillonians will, I hope, forgive me for the liberties I have taken with the topography of their beautiful islands. They will realise that, while a few of the names of places have been changed and some of the customs and rituals altered, the story is completely fictional and the characters bear no resemblance to any persons living or dead

—Margaret Gill

Acknowledgements

To both my sister Joan Holah and novelist Elizabeth Reeder for their valuable comments, Taff Lovesey, author, for his suggestions and Jimmy Paget Brown of Periglis Cottage for local observations.

CHAPTER 1

▼

With the coming of the narwhal, everything changed.

Gray Edmond made his first sighting of the tusk the day of the islands' gig race. He ought to have been down at the quay to see the island's gig team battle triumphantly through the Sound and into the main harbour, Porth Conger. All the islanders would be there.

Instead he was sitting on the rocks at the Western side of the island looking out to Bishop Rock Lighthouse which at this distance looked like a long black threatening finger pointing to the sky. The sea was as still as glass. The sun blazed down. There was not a sound. The huge black backed gulls on the jutting rocks below Periglis Bay were motionless, as if carved in wood.

He picked idly at the grey green lichen which coated everything—walls, gates, rocks—with a bristly layer. He wished he'd gone to watch the race, but even if he had gone he knew he wouldn't have been welcome. He loved the island, had lived there most of his life and yet he knew he didn't belong. He never had. The islanders had always made that clear.

He hunched forward gazing at strands of floating seaweed and flicked back his long loose hair. Dad and Robert always wore theirs in a tight pigtail but he hated the restriction.

"Yes!" he shouted shattering the silence and scaring a flock of sanderlings that took flight. He leaned forward. There was decidedly something there. In an unusual patch of iridescent green there was something long and golden shimmering in the sun's rays.

Slipping off his leather sandals he slithered down to the edge of the rocks, moved with practised skill over huge pebbles on the shore slimy with dark green weed, and waded in without a gasp at the sudden impact of icy cold seawater.

Beyond the pebbles there were patches of gritty sand and his foothold was sure as he edged towards the shining thing.

"Ouch!" He felt a strange throbbing in his arm like an electrical impulse. The patch of green was growing denser, thicker by the moment and as his hand groped down it met a gelatinous mass. Suddenly the water began to cloud over and he heard a low-pitched humming sound. It was just as though some device had been switched on. He began to wade in deeper. But he hadn't gone far before he heard someone calling him. Gray turned to see a man with grizzled beard, skin tanned a deep mahogany. He was coming down over the steep sandy bank onto the shore.

"Have you found anything, lad?"

Gray shook his head. During the violent late Spring storms the seas round Hellweather Reef had boiled with such fury that pieces of ancient wrecks had been cast up onto the shore, shards of china and occasionally old coins, beads and pieces of jewellery. But it had been months now since anything worthwhile had been washed ashore.

You might have guessed that, old Tom Jenkins. You never miss a trick round here, do you? he thought as he waded to shore keeping his thoughts to himself. He liked Tom; he was one of the few islanders who were friendly. But if he had found anything he wasn't going to tell.

"You decided against going out with your Dad fishing then?"

Gray nodded.

"But you've been out in all weathers before, and today, of all days. The sun's brilliant and there isn't a ripple in the sea."

Gray couldn't explain the sense of unease he'd felt about going out in the boat today. He'd had similar feelings the day a child was drowned swimming off Gugh island. And then there'd been the time when he was walking across Castella Down when suddenly something made him stop and turn round. A little distance from him he'd seen the figure of a sailor dressed in old-fashioned clothes, facing out to sea with his right hand held up shielding his eyes. Gray had stared at him for a few moments and then blinked in amazement as the figure disappeared from view. It was just as though he'd seen a mirage. Dad, of course, would never accept that you could know about things before they happened. And as for seeing ghosts! So he didn't speak about his feelings to anyone except Tom.

"Guess you did see a ghost, or *Renteman* as they calls 'em," he'd said. "Nothing surprises me. There must be thousands of dead men's bones and wrecks between here and the Bishop. Ye knows the proverb of the island. 'For one man who dies a natural death here, nine are drowned.' And it was just off Annett, or Bird Island, as some call it, that the *Hollandia* went down. Oh! centuries ago. But best you don't speak of seeing anything to anyone. The islanders are a surprisingly superstitious lot despite their toughness and you don't want to go stirring feelings now, do you?"

As if I would go blabbing. And who would I blab to?

"As if," was all he'd said.

But now on such a quiet day, he had to agree with Tom, his uneasiness seemed unfounded.

"I'm just going across to Burnt Island to see if I can see Dad and Rob coming back into the bay in *Minerva*," he said.

"What's that you say?"

"I'm going across the causeway to look for Dad," Gray said in a louder tone.

"Not waiting to hear how the gig boats got on then?"

But Gray was already speeding across the rocks and boulders that formed the causeway between Periglis Bay and the tiny isle that was more of a spit than anything, piled high with dark brown boulders.

It was a gloomy place where no birds nested, where no vegetation grew, where no islander would set foot. They said the ground was tainted and that it was a place where spirits roamed at nightfall. Dad couldn't abide the place but Gray loved it, it was his own private sanctuary. Nobody ever bothered him here. Only the occasional lone tourist ever ventured this far, but they never stayed.

Among the chaos of stones was a strange world of boulders and rocks shaped like prehistoric creatures of the deep, grotesquely sculpted by wind and sea. He settled down on the flank of rock shaped like a beached whale, trying to distinguish small dots on the horizon, in the hope of recognising *Minerva*, the family's fishing boat. They should have been back by now.

It felt incredibly hot. The sky was clouding over, growing ominously black. Then he felt a few angry puffs of wind which ruffled the waves and sent them surging up onto the rocks casting up a long strange ivory coloured object on to the lower reaches of half submerged rocks and shingle. Surely, this was the very same thing he'd seen in the bay, he thought as he clambered down from his perch. Above the noise of the waves he thought he heard someone calling a name, a name he thought he'd heard somewhere at some distant time. The sound of the name seemed to hiss and swish like the rush of incoming tides. Then came the same low-pitched hum he'd heard before. This time whatever it was it wasn't going to get away.

Balancing on a boulder he reached down and seized the spear-like object as the next rush of waves bore it within his grasp.

"Jeez!" he screamed. An electric current shot through his arms and legs and ran up and down his spine.

What on earth was that?

He hauled the thing up with as much speed as he could and, shoving it onto a rocky ledge, studied it while giving it a wide berth.

It must have been at least a metre long, with a regular spiral pattern running along its length and sharply pointed at the end. There were also some strange markings on it that he couldn't make out.

He guessed it was a narwhal's tusk. He'd heard they possessed magical powers. But what was it doing here?

This one certainly possessed power, but more like modern scientific power than old-fashioned magic. Could it really be a whale's tusk? He remembered seeing a photo in the window of Agnes Treverick's quayside shop showing a dead narwhal with a long tusk and the fishermen standing by it were dwarfed by the huge blotched and mottled bulk of the creature.

He thought he ought to go down to the shop to check it out but for now he should hide it. Crouching down, he pushed the tip into a deep cleft between the rocks and began easing the tusk gradually in. There was a blinding flash of sheet lightening that lit up the sea and surrounding reefs followed by an enormous clap of thunder. Then he leapt up in amazement as a dazzling globe of electrical fire exploded and he experienced a sharp shock in his right hand. Immediately spots of warm rain began to fall on his shoulders. Soon it was sluicing down and the now gusty wind was building up to gale force. If he didn't hurry the causeway would be awash and he'd have to swim across the bay. But with waves lashing up several feet he didn't fancy his chances.

He reached the shore with only minutes to spare. The causeway was now well under water and small craft in the bay were being tossed and buffeted by huge waves. There was still no sign of Dad and Rob and as he raced back home to the cottage his heart was pounding with fear.

He passed Jo Henderson, the boy from Higher Farm as he neared the top of the Downs. "You're such a wuss, Gary Edmond!" he yelled. "Why weren't ye cheering our team on at the gig race? Chickening out as usual. But they won without your support."

On any other day Gray would have stood his ground and answered back. But today, with such a rising dread filling his whole being, he had no heart to reply to the taunt.

CHAPTER 2

▼

"You'll catch your death, going around half naked in weather like this. You're like a young savage," grumbled Charlotte Jenkins, pushing a grey strand of hair from her face with a floury hand. "At least your Dad and your brother'll have their oilskins. Should have been back an hour gone, not that there's much catch these days. Crabs a-plenty but not the good fat lobsters they used to get."

Gray didn't answer. He flicked the wet out of his hair and hurried through the kitchen and up to his own room. He rushed anxiously over to his window which looked out onto St Warna's Bay. Perhaps they'd got blown off course and had pulled into St Warna's instead, although he doubted it. The coast there was too rocky. They were all used to storms on this windswept outpost of an island but this was an unusually vicious storm for September. The rain was lashing against the window in fury and the wind howling as only the wind knew how in these stretches of the Atlantic. It seemed to be carrying with it the sounds of wrecked vessels and the cries of anguished sailors.

*   *   *   *

Then there were voices down below, men's voices, strange voices. He crept to the head of the stairs and listened. It had been hours since the storm began and the family boat had still not returned. He knew without asking who the men were.

"Of course the search will go on through the night but as we received no signal from them they could be anywhere ... and in this storm."

He heard Charlotte snivelling and then the familiar voice of her husband Tom which sounded hoarse and broken. "The boy ... what about the boy?"

Yet Gray felt nothing. His whole body and mind were frozen into a strange numbness. He forced his legs to walk down to the kitchen. Both adults looked at him as though they'd seen a ghost.

"The coastguards were here a few minutes ago."

"I heard them."

"Don't worry lad, they'll turn up, right as rain."

"Yes," he said woodenly.

"They'll have taken shelter somewhere out of the storm. Your dad's a very capable man. He can handle a boat better than most and Robert's a strong lad. They'll be alright."

But they should have been back ages before the storm began. Something else must have thrown them off course. It had to have been something else. Gray couldn't get that idea out of his head. There was something so strange about the way the storm had blown up so suddenly, on such a still day when there hadn't been a breath of wind.

"If you'd like us to stay on we can," said Charlotte. "There's nothing spoiling at our cottage and now I've finished baking for the café Tom could give me a hand to set the tables and chairs out for the morning."

They were just trying to be kind. Nobody else except the Jenkins dared to defend his family's way of life. They all hated Dad just because he didn't need anyone, because he lived his own separate life, because he believed in the freedom to grow his own food, milk his own cows, run his own self-made industry, his wholefood café, his herbal soaps and handcrafted shoes and, the biggest cause of friction, educate his own kids. As the years went by the islanders' attitudes had hardened. And the general consensus appeared to be 'If they want their own freedom then let the bastards take care of themselves'.

Dad often said, "You've got to learn to be brave to live in freedom. When you try exercising even small freedoms the jackboots start marching in."

"There's no need to stay," Gray found himself saying. "I'll be alright. I can do the tables after I've seen to the animals. I need to keep busy. I know Dad'll be here soon."

"Of course he will," said Tom, casting a cautious look at his wife as if forbidding her to deny it.

"Well. if you're sure," said Tom, "we'll be off. Let us know as soon as you 'ear anything."

The storm raged throughout the night and Gray stayed watching by the window until he finally fell asleep in an armchair. In a fitful dream he thought he saw the giant narwhal emerge from the waves, its tusk shining like a beacon. It seemed to be pointing to a spot on the shore of the bay where a heap of rocks rose up taller than a house and shone like the tusk with an unearthly light. But when he awoke to a bright clear dawn sky and looked down into the bay the shore appeared empty.

Dad and Robert did not return that day. Nor on the next day, nor the next. They'd simply disappeared. The coastguards searched every inch of the Western islands and the reefs. They found no bodies and no wreckage. Yet something inside him told Gray they weren't dead. He knew he'd feel it if they were.

Some of the islanders were heartless enough to say 'good riddance' and hinted that it wasn't just the storm that had caused David Edmond and his eldest son to disappear. Only a few, more sensitive souls, expressed pity for the lone boy and wondered what would happen to him and the whole food café the family had run.

Since the bodies were never found there couldn't be a funeral. Charlottte made a wreath from bell heather and wild iris. The priest from the mainland came. He conducted a memorial service in the little stone church by the old lifeboat house attended by Charlotte, Tom and a small group of sheepish looking neighbours who'd tried to avoid the general condemnation of the Edmond family and remain neutral.

Afterwards Gray went down to the end of the old quay alone, watching the sea washing in and out, then threw the solitary wreath out into the bay.

He could feel the swirling waters like the churning waters of his belly. He could hear the music of the old world, the lost drowned world under the sea calling him, calling him, pulling him, whispering again a name that sounded like the hissing of surf rushing over pebbles. *Cass ... sss ... eras ... ides* it seemed to say. *Dive, dive, there's no escape, dive deep, plunge and return to us.* And the same throb, throbbing he'd felt when he touched the tusk filled his body, pulling him in until his whole being was one gigantic throb. It was as though he was being drawn into the waters unable to resist. As he swayed forward ready to leap he felt a firm strong hand on his shoulder. "Come lad, ye'll not bring them back by drowning ye'self. Come 'ome now."

CHAPTER 3

▼

"There *is* a will in an office in Penzance."

Mr Perry senior, of Perry and Perry, Solicitors, was as dreary looking as his ill-lit office with his old-fashioned side-whiskers and stiff collar. He was addressing the woman social worker, a brown mouse of a woman in a drab pleated skirt and off-white blouse, her hair scraped back off her forehead.

Gray sat facing them dressed in his most respectable pair of jeans and sweater impatient to be out in the fresh air, down at St Mary's Quay, sailing back home.

"But while the body ... er," Mr Perry coughed, took off his glasses and polished them on his handkerchief, "... Mr Edmond, cannot be found, the will cannot be enacted. There's no proof, Miss Morrison, no proof. Still, there's the question of ... there must be some relative who could act as guardian."

"Well, Gary?" Miss Morrison fixed the boy with her little brown beady eyes. "Is there anyone you know of?"

Gray squirmed. No one called him that any longer. His family had laughingly referred to him as Gray ever since he first misspelt his real name, Gary. He was what his father called dyslexic but he didn't care about that. Reading and writing didn't feature highly on his list of favourite things. From that moment he remained Gray, like the grey seals that swam in the bay, like the grey sea that washed in, like the grey heron and the grey plover. The name was just right. It suited him. Miss Morrison's calling him Gary only emphasised how out of step she was with him.

He shook his head and turned away, trying to see out of the window. It was difficult to believe that only a few metres away the sea was lapping up against the quay. He longed to leave, to run down to the sea and freedom, back to the rocks, to his home, his refuge.

"Even if there was someone, it would have to go before a magistrate. Temporary care would have to be arranged. And there's the question of the house. He cannot be held responsible at the age of fifteen. The Duchy will have him out. There must be someone."

Mr Perry rustled a sheaf of papers on his desk.

It was as if he'd ceased to exist, thought Gray, and had become a piece of paper, a cipher to be shifted around. He'd just lost his dad and brother and yet *they* would get him out. Who were *they*, the Duchy, the landlords, to decide what happened to him? What kind of folk were they who would do such a thing? It was his home, paid for by Dad. And no Duchy was ever going to get him out.

"Some relative," re-iterated Mr Perry. "What about the mother?"

Gray turned to look at the old man. Why all this interrogation? Why couldn't they just let him go? He had only the faintest recollection of his mother. He'd only been a baby when she left, but he knew about the bitterness, the bitterness of his father who refused to mention her ever again.

"She remarried didn't she?" said the little woman in brown. "Went to live abroad ... and then ..." She was making empathetic noises.

Was killed in a brutal senseless murder in a Kenyan jungle. Inwardly, Gray supplied the words that he'd heard from Charlotte Jenkins' lips years later when he'd grown up. It was as though it had all happened to someone else, someone he hadn't even known.

"There has to be someone who can act as guardian. There's the executrix of the will." Mr Perry coughed again. "A Miss Aleyne Golighy. We could contact her. A great aunt, I believe."

Gray shuddered without knowing why.

"And," added Miss Morrison, "probably a very old lady by now who wouldn't want to take responsibility for a boy or to come out to what she would regard as the end of the world. And then there's the question of schooling."

"No!" said Gray, uttering his first word of the afternoon. "No! Not school. No way. Anyway I'll be sixteen in October."

*   *   *   *

Miss Aleyne Golighy, commonly known to her acquaintances as Leyne, pronounced to rhyme with mean, left her Edinburgh flat with her cat, Co'burn, and caught the train for Penzance. Leyne was a historian who specialised in mediaeval history and the word 'mean' had become attached to her mainly because she never shared any of her knowledge or ever seemed to publish any erudite papers for others to read. Her reputation as a historian was founded solely on the one solitary lecture she'd given to an amateur archaeological society, now defunct. However there were many other reasons for the name. She had once been caught stealing toilet paper from a public convenience, and woe betide any child who came knocking at her door at Hallowe'en.

Travelling the 500 or so miles from Edinburgh to Penzance at Perry and Perry's expense gave her a deliciously malignant pleasure. She had no intention of looking after the brat spawned by her now late nephew, but she was relishing the thought of a holiday by the sea and the possibility of owning a house that might be converted into apartments to be profitably rented out to wealthy mainlanders. Who knows, she might even brush up her knowledge of ancient sites and give talks to visiting tourists. She rubbed her hands with glee and then stroked the ebony fur of Co'burn through the bars of his cage. The cat narrowed his yellow eyes and glared at her.

The pair arrived in Penzance in a heavy downpour and took a taxi which set them down in North Street, a narrow road running behind the main high street. Leyne, clad in a voluminous black waterproof cape, struggled out with boxes and bags and set the cat's cage down on the streaming wet cobblestones. A strong stench of fish filled the air and despite his hatred of the wet, Co'burn twitched his whiskers in pure delight.

Leyne rang the bell of a building resembling an old chapel. The brass plate by the door read Marie Merrick, astrologer and medium, consultations by appointment only. There was a scraping sound as the door was dragged open across flagstones. A young girl wearing an apron and hair tied back in a pony tail glanced curiously at the flabby faced woman before her with her long wisps of hair plastered wetly across her forehead, and then shrank back, startled by the sharply brilliant grey eyes.

"Marie's expecting me," said Leyne, bustling in, shaking pools of water from her cape and dragging in her luggage and the cat's cage. She opened the flap and to the girl's dismay a black streak of bedraggled fur shot out and up the nearest stairs.

"But she's about to take a séance ... can't see anyone," stammered the poor girl, clearly in awe of this mountain of a woman. "And the cat can't go in there," she said as Co'burn shot back down the stairs and charged through an open door and into the next room.

"Oh! He's used to such matters," was all Leyne said as she pushed her huge bulk through the door following in Co'burn's wake.

A musty damp smell mingled with a fainter odour of incense greeted her. As her eyes became accustomed to the gloom, Leyne could see two rows of elderly women seated on benches facing a kind of dais on which sat a thin bent woman, whom she recognised as her friend Marie, head sunk onto her chest as though deep in trance.

At that very moment Marie's head shot up, revealing a sharp bony face. Her eyes were glazed and she began to speak in a monotonous tone. "Someone is here from ..." the voice faded, her head sank back down. There was a long pause. One of the women began to sniff and took out a handkerchief. Leyne bent down and collared Co'burn who had slunk to the back of the room. Then there was a piercing cry seemingly from nowhere as Marie remained motionless with sunken head.

"Casseritides." The word echoed round the room. And then again in a hollow voice, the syllables came hesitantly and separately: "Cass ... eri ... tides."

The old women shuffled and hunched up as they turned round in fear. Co'burn's body went rigid and the damp fur on his back stood up on end.

"Casser ... Casser ..." The voice choked and then faded.

Marie's head jerked up. The nostrils of her long nose twitched and her face took on a startled look as she focussed on Leyne's brilliantly glittering eyes.

"Aleyne," she stammered. "I wasn't expecting you until tomorrow." She shuffled off the dais and walked over to her friend, addressing the small gaggle of women as she did. "Well ladies, I think that closes our séance for today."

"But what did it all mean, that terrible voice at the end?" asked one of them. "It wasn't your usual, Marie. It was scary, really scary."

"Yes," added another. "That scream went right through me, not your usual thing at all."

Marie appeared nonplussed. She frowned and tapped her long bony fingers together.

"What exactly happened?" she asked, appealing for help to Leyne.

"Don't you know? It's your séance," said Leyne sourly.

"Spirits speak through me to whoever is gathered here. I am simply the channel," replied Marie evasively.

Leyne shook her head in disbelief as Marie took her arm.

"Goodbye everyone," Marie said as the audience filtered out through the open door muttering disconsolately. "I'm sorry if you didn't all get the answers you were looking for tonight. Perhaps you will next week when we meet again."

*   *   *   *

"What was all that about?" asked Leyne as she shrugged off her cape and accepted the cup of tea Marie was handing her in the room that served as lounge in the sparse living quarters upstairs.

"All what?" Marie's pale blue haunted eyes looked searchingly at her.

"Look, I've known you since school days, always thought you a bit mad," said. Leyne, returning her gaze, "but this séance business tonight was like being in the chamber of horrors. Don't you really have any idea what happened?"

"No. I don't," said Marie crossly. "I've told you, I go out like a rocket when I trance. I don't hear a thing when I'm 'out'. The people who attend hear what they want to hear; it isn't my job to interpret for them. But I gather there was something special tonight."

"You could call it special. I'd say hair-raisingly special." Co'burn crept closer to his mistress' chair and rubbed his head against her legs. "I've always heard about a cat's fur standing on end but I've never seen it before tonight. I bought him years ago from a gypsy who looked more like a witch than old Mother Shipton, so I guess he's seen and heard stranger goings on in his short lifetime."

"Cats and séances should never mix," said Marie. "They have fourth dimensional vision and should always be kept away."

"It wasn't his fault the door was wide open."

"That's to let negative influences out, not to let cats in."

"Like that voice?" Leyne pursed her lips and shook her head.

"A man's, was it?" Marie gently probed.

"No. No. It sounded like no living creature. It was all hollow and then choking as though drowning."

"Then I would say that's a warning." Marie's red-rimmed eyes took on a vacant look as though she'd temporarily tranced again. "The voice was meant for you."

"For me? Why for me?"

"Who else? You're here because of a drowning."

"Or a clever disappearance. Never trusted that nephew of mine. If he was in trouble he'd always manage to wriggle out of it some way."

"Humph!" said Marie. "Why would he want to disappear? Isn't there a son? Isn't that why you're going out there?"

"Yes. I wrote you. That's where I'm going if only this wretched weather would clear."

"And you're taking him?" Marie pointed to the cat that was pawing at Leyne's skirt. "The islanders won't like it. St Hellicks is a major nesting place for migratory birds. Twitchers come from all over to catch sight of rare birds there."

"Then they'll have to lump it. Co'burn and I will never be parted."

"Take care, Aleyne. I think the voice you heard really was some kind of warning."

"Nonsense. You know I don't hold with spirits and all that stuff. But I'm sure I've heard the name, Casseritides, somewhere before." Leyne got up and began to look around the room. "Do you have something like an encyclopaedia?"

"Not exactly, but there's an old book full of the most interesting information that was left here by the parson who once ran the chapel. Now where did I put it?" Marie got down on her hands and knees and began pulling old newspapers and files from under a sideboard. "Got it," she said, triumphantly dragging out a scarred black leather book. She flicked it open. "Oh dear! I don't know if this will help. I must have been mistaken. This seems to be a historical survey of Cornwall only." She turned over several pages and then looked up in astonishment. "Ooh! Listen to this." As she began to read aloud the tone of her voice became strangely staccato and excitable. "49 degrees 55'N and 6 degrees 19'W lies Casseras. According to Plato this is the tip of the vast drowned land mass once known as Atlantis that stretched from way beyond the Azores right up to the shores of Brittanicus."

"Let me see," said Leyne, eagerly snatching the book from her friend's hands. "Casseras? I wonder."

She searched through to the back of the book and ran her thumb down the index then paused and looked up into Marie's eyes which had taken on a strange gleam.

"You've found it, haven't you?"

"Yes. 'Casseras,'" Leyne began reading aloud. "'Sometimes known as Casseritides and later as Sculla after the Roman goddess and now called 'The Scillies'. Which is exactly where I'm heading.... Casseritides."

As she closed the book Leyne was aware that her fingers had become icy cold. She knew that the unearthly voice that had uttered the name had shaken her more than she dared to admit. Yet she didn't know why.

CHAPTER 4

▼

Gray was waiting at the quay with the tractor when Leyne arrived in St Hellicks. She was hauled off the *Spirit of St. Hellicks* like a huge parcel by the burly man who collected the fares.

"They'll not take to it," he growled, flinging Co'burn's cage unceremoniously after her. "Th'islanders'll drown it as soon as look at it."

As Leyne came puffing and blowing up the steep slope from the quay following a trolley loaded with crates of produce, luggage and Co'burn's cage, Gray studied his approaching guardian. One thing was certain—she wasn't going to get in his way too much judging by the size of her. With no transport on the island except the odd tractor and scooter, she wouldn't be dogging his footsteps. But he was mystified why she had chosen to come. She'd never written to, or to his knowledge, ever spoken to Dad and he couldn't imagine that a great aunt, and a spinster at that, could have much in common with boys. And since her first words when she finally came up level with him and the tractor were "You can think again boy if you think I'm riding in that," it was clear, they were not going to get on.

"It's a long hard walk to the other side of the island, Aunt Aleyne," said Gray fastening Co'burn's cage onto the back of the tractor with the luggage and looking at the scrawny cat in dismay. What would the islanders say? A cat on an island famed for its rare birds? Weren't the Edmonds disliked enough already? Disliked because they were originally mainlanders who never mixed with the island community and who were seen as profiting from the island resources and not giving anything back in return. Well, he raged inwardly, didn't the café attract tourists who in turn spent money at the local pub and quayside shop and kept the boats busy plying between here and St Mary's, which paid the boatmen's wages? But then Gray had long ceased to wonder overmuch at the simmering hatred his family stirred. He knew his father had been a quiet man who never spoke unless spoken to and who believed in his right to live in isolation from the rest of the world. Gray had never known any other way of life or known the companionship of other boys except his older brother.

"I'll walk," said Leyne, firmly refusing Gray's offer to help her up beside him. "Just tell me the way."

Gray shrugged. *You're crazy but suit yourself. You'll learn.*

After directing her round via the coastal path he climbed back onto the tractor which chugged slowly away from the quay up the steep winding road.

He had just passed the dumpy white lighthouse and was heading round the bend towards Castella Down when he was forced to brake sharply. A group of island boys were blocking the path. Jo Henderson broke away from the rest and stepped up to the tractor.

"What ye up to wuss? What ye got there?"

He walked round to where the luggage and the cat's cage were fastened and rammed his fist viciously against the bars. The cat hissed and snarled, baring his teeth.

Jo turned to the others and a wide malevolent grin spread over his face. "He's got a bleeding stinking moggy. Let's get it." He knocked the cage onto the path, bringing down luggage and boxes with it but the lock on the cage held firm.

"Lunatic," Gray muttered between his teeth. His hand itched to slash out at the other boy as he jumped down to rescue the cage.

"Lunatic ye'self. Where'd ye come from anyway? Escaped from a loony bin all ye' family. Don't do nothing 'cept grub wi' the pigs and cows. Don't go to school. Don't know nothing. I bet you've never snogged a girl."

"Bet he kisses the pigs goodnight," called another of the boys.

"Yeh!" Jo broke into a raucous laugh. "Bet he snogs hogs." The others joined in the laughter.

Gray's hand came up in a fist. Even as it did, he could hear Dad's voice cautioning him about never reacting to the islanders' taunts, telling him it was the bully who was always the weaker. It was then he knew he *could* control it. It didn't matter what they did or said, he'd got Dad and Rob guiding him, locked up inside him.

Jo's hand shot out and grabbed his wrist hard. He pushed his face close to Gray's. "One day we'll kill ye' pigs, an' ye' stinking cat. We'll stick a knife in and hear 'em squeal."

"Come off it, Jo," said Steve Bowles, an older, thick set, stocky lad. "Let 'im go. He ain't doing nothing."

Jo released Gray's wrist and scowling turned to the rest of the group who were beginning to split up.

"An' I say he's going nowhere with that monster," Jo insisted, going back to take a final poke at the poor creature and kicking the cage into the hedge.

"And who says?" said Gray who, finally losing his cool and springing at Jo, pinned his shoulder back so strongly the other winced.

But Steve pushed between them. "Go on, scat while you can and take ye cat. Right funny looking specimen, looks as though he's been in some scraps already," he said not unkindly.

The rest of the gang had lost interest now it didn't appear there was going to be a fight and shuffled off. Jo Henderson cast a baleful look in Gray's direction and ran after them.

Just then a buggy with crab baskets on the back pulled up and Tom Jenkins dressed in oilskins slid his huge booted feet to the ground.

"What the 'ell's going on?" Tom stared at the disaster area and, hearing Co'burn mewling, glared in disbelief at the cat scrabbling madly at the bars of its cage now hanging perilously askew from a branch in the hedgerow.

"What's been happening?" Tom asked again as he helped Gray to pick up the aunt's boxes and luggage strewn across the path and rescue the cage.

"Jo Henderson," was all Gray said.

"What's that you say? Jo 'enderson? Nasty piece of work that Jo. You didn't take 'im on did ye lad?"

"No Tom. Not quite. Almost though." Gray turned to face the old man after finally securing all the baggage. "I was ready to smash his face."

"Ye Dad wouldn't 'ave liked ye to do that. Wanted ye to stay away from violence, to learn about being free of all that."

"Free!" Gray spat the word out viciously. "What's the big deal about freedom? I mean, look at it. I've got no friends. All them with Jo Henderson think I'm a loony and a sad loser. How free's that? Freedom's dull, it's boring. It makes you a freak."

"No!" Tom shook his head. "Look at ye Dad now, stuck up for 'is rights but 'e never once let 'em get to 'im, never let 'em see 'im lose 'is temper, not to my knowledge. And, 'e was sorely provoked I can tell ye. But 'e'd find a way to deflect it, 'e'd laugh at 'em. Do ye remember 'ow some o' them lads opened the crab baskets and every one of they crabs scuttled away into the ditch?"

Gray gave a wry smile. Just remembering what Dad had said made his heart tighten into a hard knot. *I just gave 'em a fruity cursing and said "I hope your toes'll be pinched by a thousand crabs every night in your dreams."* But Gray also remembered the scared look on their faces because they genuinely believed they'd been cursed. He knew that people took his Dad to be some kind of warlock; they mocked him behind his back but feared and hated him into the bargain.

"Why do they hate us Tom?"

"Don't ask me." He rubbed his chin thoughtfully. "I guess the rest of 'em thought he should've co-operated wi' 'em more. Given 'em more of a 'elping hand out like. Called 'im stuck up an' snooty an a bit weird. The others all thought we was working for the enemy, Charlotte an' me. Nah! I got on fine wi' ye Dad. 'E just didn't fit in with their rules I suppose. I reckon it's always safest to fit in, specially on an island like this. It's too small to cope wi'differences."

"If you can figure out what the rules are," said Gray bitterly. "I suppose fitting in means going to their stuffy school and to their pub. Dad said 'the school of life's the best educator.'" *But then he was a big thinker, not like me; he never thought a mean small thought in his life.*

"Don't fret. Eventually everyone fits in somewhere. Ye Dad just got on the wrong side of the islanders right from the start an' they was always afraid of him, like he 'ad some sort of power they was scared of. Oh!" Tom said, changing the subject abruptly. "I met your aunt, at least I guessed that's who she was, trudging round the coast. She looked 'ot and ready to drop, yet there she was, positively steaming with anger, swishing away at the tall grasses growing over the path with a stick."

"It was her own fault. I warned her, but she chose to walk," said Gray.

"I offered to come back for her with the tractor," said Tom. "She just gave me a look fit to kill. She's not going to be an easy lady to please."

No indeed not, thought Gray, starting up the tractor and heading off back home. He was sure both she and the cat were going to be big trouble.

As he came to the top of the hill he looked down into the bay. He saw their dinghy floating forlornly on the tide, tugging away at its moorings. Instinctively he searched among the boats bobbing about for signs of *Minerva* and then with a painful wrenching of the heart realised that she wasn't there.

CHAPTER 5

▼

"She's not stopping in Dad's room."

Gray stomped angrily into the kitchen. It was several weeks after Leyne's arrival.

"Nothing to do with me any longer," said Charlotte, folding her apron up neatly into a square and taking her coat down from behind the kitchen door.

"Well, you let her go there in the first place."

"The guest room wasn't ready, you know that, and Robert's room was too poky."

"But it's ready now and she's moving all Dad's things out, his books, his clothes, everything's out on the landing. She can't do that."

"Sorry lad, I'm not in charge." Charlotte shrugged her shoulders, pulled on her coat and placed the folded apron on the scrubbed deal table with an air of finality. "From this moment Shearwater Farm doesn't have a housekeeper. I'm dismissed."

"What!" Gray stared at the old woman in dismay. "Why? I mean ... when? By whom?"

"Your aunt dismissed me this morning; said she'd be taking charge from now on."

"But you've always looked after everything. Dad relied on you. I rely on you now. You can't just leave." Gray went over to her, trying to look into her face but she turned away from him. "Charlotte, look at me," he demanded. "What's going on? Who'll look after the café?"

When she raised her head Gray was aware of tears in the kind brown eyes and how tired and old she looked. She took out a handkerchief and wiped the tears away. "There'll be no café from now on. Your Aunt says it doesn't pay. She's planning to turn it into a self-contained flat to be rented out. Much more profitable, she says."

"We'll see about that." Gray turned and strode towards the door.

"Don't make things worse, lad. She's a hard woman and she won't even listen to you if you're all worked up."

"But what'll you do? You'll only have Tom's earnings from the farm and the sale of the crabs."

Charlotte bit her lips and looked at him blankly for several moments as though struggling to find the words.

"She's told Tom she won't be needing him after this week." The words came out now between gasps.

"The bitch."

"No! Stop that! You oughtn't to speak like that."

"Bitch, bitch, flaming bitch … Who'll look after the animals then?"

Charlotte looked down at her hands and twisted her fingers.

"Me?" said Gray with dawning horror. "You mean me? But Tom did the work of two men … how can I….?"

"She says she's going to turn it all into a tourist attraction for visitors, thinks they'll come flocking over to see how self suffi-

ciency works and she's going to do maps for a farm trail for children."

"And which is going to run ... just like that, all on its own?"

"No, lad ... all on *your* own, that's what she intends. Tom'll
lend a hand, you know that, but we'll be hard pushed to help
much." And the tears that had been held in check began to flow
down her cheeks freely.

Gray rushed out of the room and bounded up the stairs two
at a time closing his ears to Charlotte's protests. He swore to
himself as he stumbled over a pile of books heaped on the top
step and finding Dad's door closed banged on it furiously.

As the door swung open he saw his aunt in a black woollen
dress buttoned up to the neck. She pulled herself up stiffly and
Co'burn sprang at him hissing and spitting.

"Well? What is it Gary? Where are your manners banging
like that on my door?"

"It isn't your door," said Gray, pushing the cat off with his
foot. "And my name's Gray."

Aunt Aleyne's eyes glittered dangerously. "I don't wonder.
Naturally one wouldn't expect anyone brought up like a wild
animal to be able to spell his own name. Now what did you
want?"

It was just as if there *was* a wild animal inside him wanting
only to claw and tear her. All the passion in his strong young
body surged through him as he brushed past the huge soft
flabby woman and charged into the room.

"You ... you've sent away my only friends, you've ... you've
messed with my Dad's things," Gray spluttered, incoherent
with anger.

He looked around at the room littered now with the aunt's
possessions. His anger caught in his throat as his eye lighted on

the one object, the only object not yet disposed of, Dad's old sou'wester still hanging from the back of a cane chair. Gray went over to the chair and taking the yellow oilskin in his hands crumpled it up as a feeling of utter desolation swept over him. It was so final, so devastatingly final. He knew for the first time that Dad was never coming home.

*   *   *   *

He walked out of Dad's room, ignoring his aunt and the still spitting cat, clasping the old sou'wester in his hands and went down the lane onto the shore at Periglis. He stumbled blindly over the rocky causeway, the salt of his tears and the sea spray stinging his eyes, to the familiar rocks, which were now his home, his hideaway, his secret place, his rescue, his balm, and gingerly drew the narwhal tusk out of the cleft where he'd stowed it. To his amazement the thing was now as quiet and peaceful as a baby.

He sat for a long while on a low boulder cradling it and gazing down through the emerald green waters, then out across the expanse of sea stretching right to the edge of the world, or the beginning of a new world. He wondered at that particular thought. Why a 'new world'? He considered the tusk lying across his lap. If this *was* a narwhal tusk it must have come from a much, much older world judging by the strange markings on it.

He decided to find out more. In Agnes Treverick's quayside shop there were all kinds of old books, pictures and drawings about the sea. And after all, he had all the time in the world. Let his aunt find out for herself what it was like to pump her own water and milk a cow, although he knew in his heart Old Tom wouldn't neglect to look to the cows whether he was being paid to or not.

He pushed Dad's sou'wester deep inside the cleft where he felt it would be safe and, holding the tusk like a staff, returned the way he'd come, then crossing over the old cricket pitch made his way to the quay.

The day was remarkably still and hot for late September and Gray shook the perspiration from his forehead. His long loose hair felt damp on his neck. There were still clumps of yellow trefoil, pin cushions of fading purple thrift and chamomile by the coastal path reminding him there would be no more forays with his brother searching for wild herbs for Dad's tinctures and oils. That source of income would dry up immediately if Aunt Aylene persisted in closing the café. It was on the shelves by the counter that they displayed the many coloured bottles of oils and handmade soaps for sale.

For the first time Gray regretted not learning more about the skills while he had the chance. Although both he and Robert had learnt how to cut and sew the fine leather brought over from the mainland and how to finish the handmade sandals, "Ecological Shoes" was how they were advertised, he hadn't the heart to go back into Dad's shed. Not yet; the pain was too raw for him to be there alone with all Dad's tools, surrounded by the familiar smell of leather and the fragrant smell of beeswax.

His thoughts were broken into by two fishermen returning to their boats in the bay who looked at him in an odd way. He realised the object of curiosity must be the tusk he was carrying and decided it would be wise to hide it from prying eyes. He stopped halfway up the slope to the shop and hid the tusk in the rough grass under the tamarisk hedge, taking care to pull up some tall ferns and flatten them down over the top. A thrush with speckled breast flew up alarmed as he continued up the path. It struck him as odd. The island birds were never afraid of him or indeed other humans. Visitors often remarked how amazing they found it to see birds walking along beside them as though they were going with them for a walk. By the quay, he was puzzled as two thrushes and a flock of sparrows took flight at his approach. It was so unusual he almost forgot his mission.

*   *   *   *

The shop whose paintwork was blistered and peeling was only a wooden shack. It bore the name Quay-Side Shop and underneath, in bold black lettering, 'Agnes Treverick—Proprietor'. In the window was a collection of postcards advertising second-hand bargains of 'valuable marine objects for connoisseurs'. In the centre a mangy stuffed puffin occupied pride of place. It was surrounded by a varied bric-a-brac of shells, framed photos of swarthy oarsmen, winners of historic gig races brandishing cups and trophies, a sea captain's braided hat next to a pair of binoculars described as having come from the wreck of Sir Cloudesley Shovell, various tattered marine charts and a ship's bell. Agnes was an old woman with a brood of seafaring sons and grandsons who ferried tourists, went out in the fishing boats and brought multifarious treasures home. The sound of her voice, even when she was alone in the shop could be heard shrilly itemising the goods and always with a note of exasperation.

But the object of Gray's interest was in the flyblown picture, half hidden by the puffin, of a narwhal which had been hauled up on to the quay, its vast tusk jutting sword-like into the surrounding crowd of spectators. If anyone knew anything about such things it would be Agnes, but he knew from Robert that she could intimidate the bravest into buying what they neither wanted nor could afford.

He went up to the door and gave it a shove which it resisted until he gave it a further forceful heave. As it flew open a bell clanged in the distance. A dusty black mechanical cormorant hanging from the ceiling flapped wings like an old umbrella, in his face.

It was dark inside after the brightness of the day and there was no sign of the owner. But as he leaned over to look at the contents in the window he was startled by a sharp voice demanding, "Well, don't stand there. Are you buying or selling?"

A grey haired woman with a wizened face emerged from the shadowy depths of the shop.

Gray shook his head.

"I see. Just wasting my time."

"I might have something to sell. I just wanted to ask you about ... narwhal tusks. Are they valuable?"

"Could be." She peered at him, narrowing her eyes. "You're that boy from Shearwater, aren't you? Never had nothing to do with your lot."

Gray bridled but realising he wasn't going to get any information if he showed annoyance persisted with, "Are they valuable?"

"Is it a narwhal you're telling me about?"

"Sort of."

"Well, is it or isn't it? Here!" She pushed a piece of paper across the counter and a pencil. "Draw it!"

Gray knew how to draw—it was his one real talent. He rapidly sketched the tusk and trying to see the shape of the symbols in his mind's eye drew them as he remembered them.

When he'd finished he pushed the paper back across the counter to the old woman.

"Humph!" she grunted. "How long? Length counts in these matters."

Gray stretched out his arms.

"Aha," she said. "Fifty pounds."

Gray was silent, unsure how to reply

"Well," she hesitated, "if you're right about the markings they could be hundreds, nay, thousands of years old, done by them Icelanders, I guess, so maybe a hundred pounds."

"A hundred for an old tusk?"

"Where'd you find it?" The old woman came close up to him and stared up at him greedily. "I could get you a good price for it. Well! Do you have it or not?"

Gray felt a sudden chill. It wasn't his to sell. It didn't seem like the kind of thing you sold. It had come to him from the sea. It was a treasure, not something to be bartered. He'd only wanted to be sure what it was. What if the Treverick brothers got wind of it?

"No! No! I just read about one like that," he lied, feeling her eyes searching his. And, knowing she didn't believe him, a hot flush of embarrassment rose on the back of his neck.

"Always knew you was weirdos at Shearwater. Go on! Get outa here … wasting my precious time."

And Gray fled, leaving the tusk where it was, hidden under the hedge, thinking to retrieve it after dark.

CHAPTER 6

▼

Later that day Gray stood on the shore at Periglis looking out to sea, pondering on the conversation with Agnes Treverick and the wisdom of hiding the tusk so near to the shop. The sea was quiet and the small craft in the bay drifted lazily, creating a sense of calm that he was far from feeling. He couldn't dismiss an underlying unease. When he'd first found the tusk its energy and power had surprised, even shocked him, and now its quietness felt somehow ominous, unnatural.

He noticed Tom hauling the wooden keepbox, in which he kept his catch, onto the deck of his boat, *Sea Rover*, checking that all was well and then lowering it back just below the surface of the water. Gray watched as Tom pulled his dinghy alongside and got in and then he ran over to the old quay to wait while Tom rowed across the bay, tied up and clambered up the stone steps bringing with him an oily, fishy smell. Gray noticed the old man was breathing heavily and seemed out of sorts.

"Eh lad, something's disturbing the fish. Seen scores of 'em threshing around in whirlpools, as though they'd gone crazy."

"Could be the weather. Blazing heat one day, storms the next," Gray ventured.

"Nah! It's something more'n that." Tom wiped his brow, sat down heavily on a pile of wooden crates and gazed into the distance, his eyes half closed, as though he was fathoming sea secrets from deep inside himself. Then he sighed and shook his head. "Nay, 'tis something very odd, lad."

Gray sat down beside him. Tom knew so much about the sea but he seemed very disturbed. "Is this the first time you've seen them behaving like this, Tom?"

"No, no, there's many a thing can upset them in these waters. Sometimes you'll see a whole shoal of mackerel whirling around as if they was inside a washing machine and that's usually 'cos there some predator around at the time. No, but this were something different, can't say rightly what's going on. They was tossing up in the air like ... like they was dolphins."

"Charlotte told me ..." Gray said, suddenly changing the subject to the one troubling him most and then stopped, wishing he hadn't bothered.

"I know what's eating ye. 'Tisn't yer fault if yer aunt decides to manage things on 'er own. Now don't ye go fretting yeself. We'll cope alright. Sometimes things that look bad turn out alright in the end."

They were both silent for some time. There was just the sound of the waves breaking gently on the shore, the knocking of the mainsail on Tom's boat in the light breeze and the distant mewling of gulls.

"I'm going to be 'elping out till the end of the week, mebbe longer. And look, I've got to take all 'er leaflets and posters across to St Mary's in the morning. Who else is she going to get to do that for 'er, eh? P'raps she'll change her mind. Don't ye fret."

Gray shook his head.

"She won't, not her," he said, wondering about the posters. Then he remembered how he'd overheard his aunt on the phone talking to someone about her forthcoming talks in the island church hall about ancient burial sites. Who would be interested anyway? He guessed she didn't know as much about such things as Dad. He was always going on about earth energies and ancient stones.

Tom looked up. The sky was turning red and the sun dropping down over the horizon like a huge orange ball.

"Didn't I see you earlier, crossing the causeway carrying something? A stick, wasn't it?"

"No. A tusk, a narwhal's tusk. It was washed up." There seemed no point in hiding it from Tom any longer. Anyway, it suddenly didn't seem all that important now. "It had some markings on it. I went to the shop to ask about it."

"Markings? Was they natural or cut in?"

"Cut in, very deep, maybe a long, long time ago I think."

"Didn't let 'er in the shop see it, did ye? Could be valuable. And ye know them Trevericks, if they gets wind of it. Sell their own soul to the devil they would."

"No, I didn't show it to her. I hid it. I was just asking her like, nothing more."

"Well, keep it that way ... they's the worst kind of scavengers, that lot."

"I was thinking of hiding it in the barn for the time being."

"Good idea, outa the aunt's way as well." Tom sucked in his cheeks and blew out a strong seaweedy smell.

Samphire, thought Gray, wrinkling his nose. The islanders often cooked the juicy leaves of the 'sea cabbage' as it was known, or an old salt like Tom often chewed the plant raw.

"Some folks do say as a beached narwhal brings bad luck to an island," continued Tom. "Was one of them many years ago and a mint of trouble it brought, drownings, and orphaned kids and poor 'arvest at sea. And I've 'eard tales of sailors finding tusks and saying 'ow there's some kind of power in them … and that they's the worst kind of luck. But nah! That's all superstition to my mind. Still, keep it outa the way."

"Yes, I will. Don't you believe in any of the tales?"

"What? Like the power?"

"Yes. Must be a sort of magic, mustn't it, if it has the power to cause things to happen?"

"That's only if folks believe it. A lot o' things are caused just by folks believing in 'em. I'd rather not meddle with such things."

"But what if it's true? When I first found the tusk it seemed sort of alive."

"Alive?"

"Alive, like in an electric current. Then when I went back to get it, it had gone dead … just as though the current had been switched off."

Tom, resting his elbow on his knee, cupped his chin in a gnarled hand and sucked in his cheeks again as though thinking about this.

"It's like Charlotte says, you spend too much time on your own. Imagination, that's all it is."

"Or, something real, something scientific?" said Gray, looking serious.

"What? Got me there."

"You know. Dad told us about St Hellick's being the tip of the ancient continent of Atlantis and how its people were so technologically advanced that in the end technology became their master. When they could no longer control it the whole land blew itself to bits or was drowned or something."

Tom laughed. "And ye think this is a bit of it? And that these islands once belonged to that place, what'd ye call it?"

"Atlantis."

"If I remember rightly, these islands wasn't called Atlantis, Casser … Casserus … something like that. And why 'adn't no-one found such things before in all them thousands and thousands of years?"

"Maybe they have, many times over. What about those sailors' tales?"

"Nah lad, I've told ye. Folks'll believe anything if ye put it into their 'eads. Strikes me folks don't really ever figure things out for themselves, they just get carried away by 'earing things and then they'll swear as they thought of it themselves, 'twas their own idea in the first place." He paused and gazed out to sea, then turned back to meet Gray's eyes staring into his own. "Now think on. If Matt Treverick and gang knows you've got a precious piece of narwhal they'll not be stopping ye next to ask ye the time o' day."

"I know, you're right, and I'll go back to get it as soon as it's dark."

*   *   *   *

The moon was huge and eerie. A harvest moon, thought Gray, staring out of his bedroom window, unable to sleep. It was too big, too strange, sort of controlling and magnetic. Still tinged with the yellow of the sun, it cast a shimmering path of light across the surface of the sea.

"Gary!"

Someone was calling him. He peered into the garden below but could see no-one.

"Gary!"

The voice sounded rough. It wasn't Tom's voice. He never called him that and he guessed Tom would be snug in his own bed in Bay Cottage. Tom sometimes fished at night but he never went out to sea in moonlight. "Scares the fish away, strong moonlight," he always said.

"Gary Edmond!"

The voice was louder—it would wake Aunt Aleyne. He opened the window and peered out into the yard below. A stocky figure stepped out of the shadows. He shrank back as he saw Matt Treverick looking up at him.

"Where've ye hid it? Ma said ye'd found something on the shore. All flotsam's ours."

"Didn't say I'd found anything," Gray hissed, pressing back against the wall. "I was only asking."

"Asking, my foot! We'll get ye Edmond if ye're lying. We'll be after ye." Matt raised his fist and shook it.

Gray shivered, drew the curtains and went back to bed but couldn't sleep. Matt's voice was still echoing in his head. "We'll be after ye, after ye." He felt certain the gang would be creeping around in the barn, climbing the loft and discovering the tusk in its hiding place under the hay. His head throbbed. He clasped his hands over it to try to stop it. "It's not yours, it's ours, ours." He thought he could still hear Matt's voice grating in his head.

"No," he said "No."

The noise in his head grew louder. It was no longer in his head, it was all around him, in the room, outside the house.

The door to his room was flung open. His aunt stood there with Co'burn at her side. The cat's eyes loomed yellow in the unearthly light, jaws apart, hissing and spitting.

"The noise," she croaked.

What? Had she heard it too?

"I thought I heard someone calling your name, shouting and cursing and waking everyone up. Get dressed at once and go and see what's going on."

"But it's the middle of the night." Gray compressed his lips in anger. This was so unreasonable.

"Do you expect me to go, boy? It wasn't my name they were shouting. Just go and see what's going on."

As if on a command the cat sprang at him.

"Get off, you beast." Gray shoved the animal away, shut the door in his aunt's astonished face and, pacing up and down, furiously kicked a half-finished sandwich, the remnant of a solitary supper, across the room.

He pulled on his jeans and a sweater. The noise was still in his head but was now less of a throb and more of a strangely familiar humming. Where had he heard that humming before?

The tusk, of course.

He went out through the yard, beyond the house. It could have been daylight, it was so light. There were ghostly shadows and he was fearful that Matt and his gang might be hiding, waiting to pounce. But there was no sign of anyone. He trod cautiously until he reached the barn, lifted the latch and suddenly the humming grew less intense. It was almost as though it was responding to his presence. How bizarre was that?

He wormed his way past the warm, heavy shapes of slumbering cows, smelling their herby breath. They stirred sleepily, opening lazy eyes as he clambered up into the hay loft. His arm snaked in under the hay and as his fingers made contact he felt again a stinging electric current that made him gasp. He withdrew his hand sharply. Then, just as suddenly as it had started, the humming ceased. Everything became peaceful, broken only by the deep, rhythmic breathing of the cattle.

His aunt was waiting standing by the door to the house in her outdoor coat.

"Well?"

"Some machinery wasn't switched off," he said, avoiding her eyes. "It was one of the lads from Lower Farm came to warn me."

She glared, looking as though she didn't believe a word.

"You'll be in charge next week ... so don't let this happen again. Do you hear?"

Gray glowered back at her and slid by without replying.

CHAPTER 7

▼

Walking over towards the Downs to bring the cows back for milking the next day, Gray thought he saw Matt Treverick climbing the stile on the top field. He'd no intention of running into Matt after last night.

He doubled back towards the farm, cut through the potato field and ran down the hill to Post Office Lane which ran parallel to the Downs. The lane was shaded by trees on either side, forming a deep culvert, tunnel-like and eerie. He knew he wouldn't be seen until he reached the edge of the field where the cows were grazing.

It was a gloomy place. Tree roots grew along the path ready to trip up the unwary. The only light was green and sepulchral. The path sloped down becoming more treacherous underfoot but Gray knew every inch of it like the back of his own hand. Suddenly his ears picked up the cracking of twigs and he was aware that there was someone ahead. A mass of shadows loomed up before him. His throat constricted—the path was blocked. A shape detached itself from the mass.

"Edmond, ye got something belongs to us."

Gray recognised Jo Henderson's voice.

There was no point in trying to confront them. There was only one thing to do. Gray plunged through the hedge, tore across the bulb field, making a beeline straight down the long scooped out earth channels between the planted bulbs, down to the edge of the field. He hurtled down the bank, aware of scampering feet behind him. If only he could reach Cove Vean before them. There were rocks there with such deep clefts he could slip into to hide—they'd never find him if he could only get there first. He could hear them yelling; they must be catching up but he didn't dare to glance back. The whole hue and cry must be after him by the sound of it. He threw himself into the deep bracken without waiting to follow the path and slid down into the little sandy cove to see Charlotte bent double on the shore, a wicker basket by her side, gathering the thick juicy stems of samphire. She looked up alarmed as he slithered on the wet stones jumping from one seaweedy boulder to another.

Any moment he expected the thump of his pursuers fists in his back. Then at last he was able to leap forward onto the shingle and with one bound clear the Jenkins' white slatted garden fence. The cottage stood on the bank at the edge of the cove. If only Tom was home. He hammered on the door.

Rod Treverick, Matt's younger brother, came up as far as the fence but hesitated to enter the gate as the others came up panting behind him. "We'll get ye, Edmond. Matt says ye've got summat that belongs rightly to us gang."

"I've nothing that belongs to you," said Gray, turning to face them as Tom opened the door.

"Marine jetsam's ours by rights, ye know that. If ye don't give it up, ye're dead."

Charlotte came up from the shore wiping her hands on her skirts and pushed through the boys assembled by her gate. "Get off wi ye the lot of ye. What fibs, we've no jetsam o' yours."

"Clear off!" came Tom's voice loud and authoritative.

Rod gave the gate an almighty kick. "Ye're going to regret this Edmond." Then he stormed off and, followed by the rest of the gang, disappeared into the shadow of the trees at the edge of the cove.

"What's going on?" said Charlotte, looking puzzled.

"Nothing to worry about," said Tom. "'e should keep outa the way of them Trevericks. I've told 'im. Did ye 'eed my warning about 'iding the tusk, lad?"

"Yes, but Matt came round last night and started threatening."

"And they'll not give up, lad."

"I don't know what ye're on about," said Charlotte, "but they's such devils and their Ma encourages them to get up to such tricks."

"Not tricks, Charlotte, that shop of theirs is full of all sorts of contraband stuff. More than 'alf of it snaffled from wrecks afore the customs can get their 'ands on it," added Tom.

"Well, don't let's all stand here. Come on, I've got some of ye favourite blackberry tart," said Charlotte, ushering Gray into the kitchen of the cottage.

Gray sat down at the table eying the huge slice of pastry oozing the dark red juice of plump blackberries that Charlotte was doling out, but his mind was still whirling.

"Tuck in then. I guess that aunt of your'n isn't feeding ye too well."

"She cares more about the cat than me."

"An' that cat'll be bringing her sorrow, mark my words," said Charlotte, pouring thick creamy custard over Gray's tart.

Tom watched the boy thoughtfully. "When ye've finished I've got something interesting in the other room to show ye. Okay, better still, bring that pie along wi ye."

But Gray scooped up the rest of the pie in one giant mouthful before following him.

"I've kept this newspaper cutting for years," said Tom, opening a sideboard drawer and handing Gray a sheet of yellowing paper.

Gray glanced at the headline. 'The Narwhal's Mysterious Tusk' and struggled to read the creased and mottled page ... 'For centuries the tusk of the narwhal has fascinated and baffled. Narwhal tusks, up to three metres long, were sold in the past as unicorn horns, often for many times their weight in gold, since they were supposed to possess magical powers. Elizabeth I had a tusk valued at £10,000—the cost of a castle. Once the German national debt was paid off with two tusks and the Hapsburgs had one made into a sceptre and had it encrusted with diamonds.'

Gray stopped reading and looked at Tom who was grinning widely. "There's more still in that article that makes ye understand the Treverick's interest, isn't there now?"

"But the vibrations and the noise it makes," said Gray. "It can't be a normal tusk."

"What's that you say? Anyways," said Tom, "it won't 'urt if I gives out in the pub that ye've come across a rusty piece of metal only fit for the scrap yard. Bob Stirling, Jed Bowles and Mary Stokes is always in the pub of a Friday night for their weekly fish and chip supper and Mary'll tell Agnes for sure."

"Thanks, Tom, but I reckon you really ought to see it first."

"What? Nah, too busy right now."

Gray guessed it was only an excuse not to meet Aunt Aleyne outside of work hours.

"Did you get all them posters done, Tom?" called Charlotte.

"What's that Charlotte?" said Tom, cupping his ear.

"She's asking if you did all the posters," said Gray.

"Aye, not that they'll bring in any custom."

Gray was all attention. He'd overheard Aunt Aleyne talking about how she was planning to do some talks but he hadn't seen the contents of the posters. "Do you have any left?" he asked Tom as they returned to the kitchen.

"Here's one I didn't manage to place. The butcher on St.Mary's said his window was too full of ads already."

> *'Series of Lectures on the Earth Mysteries*
> *and ley paths of the islands,*
> *followed by discussion on*
> *St Hellick's as the 'Casseritides'*
> *of the ancient Romans.*
> *First talk to be held in the Old Church Hall St Hellick's.*
> *3.00 p.m Saturday October 7th'*

"That's it," said Tom. "That's the name I told you about, lad, yesterday. Casserus or something like that."

"What's she know about St Hellick's?" snorted Charlotte.

"Aleyne Golighy, historian and lecturer," said Gray, quoting Mr. Perry, the solicitor. "She's brought a heap of books with her and I think she's quite famous," he added, although after he'd said it he reddened slightly, knowing he was making that up just to impress.

"She won't get anyone to come at this time of year. Next month all we'll see over here'll be bird watchers, twitchers and the like. Some interest they'll take in ancient history," said Charlotte, placing a second slice of tart on Gray's plate.

But Gray felt an unusual throb of excitement that had nothing at all to do with blackberry tart or even the narwhal but everything to do with that word Casseritides. Where had he heard it before?

CHAPTER 8

▼

"He's sulky and downright rude," Leyne said. She was talking on the telephone in the alcove between the farm kitchen and sitting room. "And Co'burn hates it here."

"I told you it was a mistake taking him."

"Perhaps. But I'm worried about the trouble Gary's stirring. There was someone shouting and cursing him last night outside the house and when I called in the Post Office today people stopped talking and pointedly ignored me."

"Was that Gary's fault?" The voice at the other end of the phone was Marie's, the Penzance astrologer.

"What do you mean?" Leyne sounded angry.

"The Edmonds have never had a good press, have they? Your coming won't change that."

"That's exactly what I do intend to change."

"Oh?"

"Right now this is a backwater, no life, nothing, utter stagnation. I'm going to bring new blood into the place. I've closed the café."

"Oh! Why?"

"It was losing money. And I've sacked the housekeeper. I can manage this house without her. I've got plans, Marie. Big plans."

"But will they work?"

"Of course. When I've made up my mind … Ooh! Forgot to tell you, I've booked the church hall for the first of my talks next Saturday."

"Good luck, hope you know what you're taking on. My hunch says you've got to watch that boy, he's trouble. What's he up to right now?"

"Off somewhere on his own, as usual."

"Watch him, Leyne, I see big trouble ahead."

"You're so negative Marie. Ooh! …" Leyne banged the receiver down as Co'burn leapt up off a chair and shot out through the open door.

He sprang between Tom's legs who was moving chairs and tables out of the café and knocked over the sign which read 'Cafe now Closed for Refurbishing.'

"Dratted animal, ye near 'ad me down." Tom cursed the cat under his breath as it ran off through the yard and headed towards the Downs.

"Co'burn, Co'burn!" yelled Leyne. But the cat, as though summoned by an invisible Pied Piper, had vanished from sight.

*   *   *   *

Gray was idly throwing stones at some recent pebble pyramids that the campers had left on the beach below Castella Down. Why did they do it? Someone started it years ago and the beach was now completely jam-packed with pebble statues. Building them had become a kind of ritual like walking the stone maze up on the Down. You found visitors walking the maze in a profound sort of trance as though they were involved in some magic rite or other. True, there was something magic about this part of the island. If you stood at the very top of Castella you could just see the strange outcrop the islanders called the 'Nag's Head'. It stood over three metres high, surrounded by a stone circle. Its humped back and hugely projecting head was awesome. Gray had always felt it resembled a fallen angel with neck outstretched and wings furled gazing out across St. Warna's bay, longing to be free to fly back home. Yet today, from this distance, it looked black and threatening, like a monster waiting to tear its prey apart. He didn't know why that thought had come into his head just then.

There was a sudden movement and angry snarl. Gray turned to see an animal marooned on top of a promontory jutting out to sea and whose base was thick with brambles. The creature was trying to shake a bramble twig out of his fur. Surely it was Co'burn! What was he doing here? Co'burn never left the house without Aunt Aleyne. Something must have scared him to make him scramble up through a thorn hedge. He was scrabbling madly to dislodge the thorns on his back and was in danger of plummeting to his death.

Gray hacked at the bramble thicket with a large stone and forced his way through, expecting the animal would fly at him. But as he stretched out a hand to dislodge the thorns, the creature remained quite still and then to his surprise sidled up to him and rubbed his back against Gray's legs. Such a change in the cat's nature made him wonder if this was indeed Co'burn. But there was no doubt it was him judging by the singular ginger stripe behind the ear. Gray felt an unusual tremor in his hands and a warmth coursing down his arm as he carefully removed the thorny twig, still wondering how a demon cat could become so tranquil.

He'd better get him home. He knew Aunt Aleyne wouldn't be long in accusing him of enticing the cat to the edge of the sea to drown him. But it was going to take some coaxing to get the animal back down safely. Gray bent to pick the cat up, amazed how docile it had become. It was quite a nice cat after all, he decided as he cradled the animal in his arms and pushed his way back down.

As he reached the camp field the cat began to claw frantically at his arms. Gray heard a humming sound and felt a strange vibration that churned his stomach, making him want to retch. The cat went rigid. The sensation lasted no more than a few seconds and then the humming ceased. Then there was silence broken only by the gentle lapping of waves on the shingle by the campsite. Co'burn, sensing home and safety, leapt out of his arms and shot back up the farm path.

Gray noticed Tom coming out of the farmyard, heading for the barn, and he wondered if Tom had heard anything.

$$* \qquad * \qquad * \qquad *$$

When Gray came into the yard he was hailed by Tom who was looking unusually serious.

"Did ye look in on the cows before ye went off a-wandering?" he asked.

Gray was surprised by the hard edge on Tom's voice.

"No, sorry. You weren't expecting me to drive them up to the top field today. I remember you saying you'd do it."

"Oh aye! An' I did that, between moving all the extra tables and chairs from the café that she didn't want *and* carting 'em by tractor down to the pub *and* persuading the landlord they'd be fine for extra seating in the pub garden."

"Seems she really means to turn it into a flat then?"

Tom sighed as he guided Gray towards the barn. "I want ye to look at one of the cows. I think she's real sick."

The cow lay motionless and she didn't raise her head as they pushed open the barn door.

"I thought at first it was 'er leg and I'd get Jed Rowe up to look at 'er, and that mebbe she just needed 'oofing. They cows've not been done this season, and I reckoned that was the trouble. But between 'elping yer aunt I didn't get time"

"Oh."

Gray knew Jed made a regular call to 'hoof' the cows but hadn't since his Dad had disappeared. He always thought of it like an in-depth pedicure, poking out all the ingrained small stones to prevent the cows going lame.

"When I finally got round to looking at 'er I got to worrying it was something worse."

"Like?"

"Well, she was slobbering something bad, didn't milk and both legs looked real sore."

Gray went over to the cow and stretched out his hand and patted her back.

"Poor thing."

The moment he touched her he felt a heat and a tingling travelling down his arm into his hand just like he'd experienced with Co'burn. The cow stirred, opened its eyes and blinked and then got up, and stood strongly and firmly on its legs.

"If I 'adn't just seen that I'd not 'ave believed it," said Tom. "That cow was as sick as could be. No ways could I 'ave persuaded 'er to get up." He bent down to inspect her legs. "Not a blessed sign of soreness ... I must be dreaming. What did ye do to 'er, lad?"

"Don't know, Tom. I just don't know."

"I felt a kind of wind on my back when ye touched 'er, an' there's not a whisper of breeze in the air today." Tom shivered and pursed his lips. Then clearly deciding to make light of it, said, "Ye Dad was good with all 'is animals. Ye must 'ave got 'is gift, lad."

But Gray was puzzled. He looked up into the hayloft wondering.

CHAPTER 9

▼

During the next few days Gray was kept busy helping Tom to finish clearing the café and moving all the furniture from Rob's room into it.

"We need the money, lad, Charlotte and me. Otherwise I wouldn't be doing such an 'urtful thing to ye."

"And that's the only reason I'm helping. Do you think I'd be doing it for her? She's already taken over Dad's room and now all Rob's things, his radio, his books, his bed; everything's going to be used by strangers. It hurts so much I could kill her."

"Nah! I don't think so," said Tom, placing a hand on the boy's shoulder. "All I say is, ye're worth a dozen of 'er. Think what pride ye dad would 'ave 'ad in the way ye dealt with that sick cow. She was up and better in a day and back grazing with the 'erd. She's as right as rain now. 'ow ye did it beats me. If I didn't know better I'd say there was some magic at work."

But Gray shrugged off the hand impatiently. He not only didn't want to talk about it, he didn't even want to think about it. When Dad and Rob went to sea that day he knew something was going to happen. He'd felt it like a black hand clutching at his heart. All those times when he'd known something was going to happen he wanted to run away from the terrible responsibility of knowing. And now the idea that he'd done something even more incredible terrified him.

"The café's going to make a right comfortable flat with all the extras ye dad put in, like the microwave in the kitchen and the shower in the washroom," said Tom. "All that'll be left to do will be tidying up the garden."

"What garden?" Gray scoffed. It was just a tiny patch of overgrown weeds with a few bedraggled agapanthuses shedding the last of their sky blue petals.

"You'll see. It'll take me next to no time to get it in trim. Can't go on calling it the café though, can we?"

"I heard her saying over the phone to someone that it was going be called the Shearwater Flat."

"Aye, that's not a bad name for it. Not that it'll matter to me come Saturday."

"There'll still be lots of work to do, more than I can handle. I can't think why she doesn't realise it."

"No! Once I've got the church 'all ready for 'er talks she'll not be needing me any more."

"Aunt asked you to do that as well?"

What cheek, thought Gray. But how like her. She just used people and then cast them off, like old rags; first it was Charlotte and now Tom. But this was the last time she was going to use him.

"What about the cows and the rest of the animals?"

"She'll sell them." Tom put down the bookshelf he was carrying and wiped the sweat off his face with his sleeve. "I understood 'er to say as she is going to concentrate on rentals of the flat only. I gather she thinks it could bring 'er in a fair sum. So she's given up the idea of the farm trail."

Gray winced.

"Sorry lad! I know this must all be very painful for ye, but what'd she do wi' livestock anyway? She's not going to live the life you Edmonds did, is she? Prefers 'er food outa tins and packets, don't she? Look 'ow quickly she got rid of my Charlotte who never touched tinned food in 'er life. Good 'ome cooking and natural like, is Charlotte."

Gray sighed, remembering the blackberry tart.

"Well, I'll just put this bookshelf up behind the settee where she wants it and then I'll be off. I see that cat of 'ers is back … dratted creature near 'ad me down on my back, and me carrying that load of chairs. Couldn't make out what on earth was up wi'it. Do ye know what was eating it?"

Gray shook his head although he was pretty sure he knew. It was odd how no-one else had picked up the pulsating sound made by the tusk. It was almost as though the sound occurred at a deeper or maybe higher level than normal hearing. He knew that bats and other creatures responded to very high frequencies humans couldn't hear. He shivered, suddenly realising what that meant.

CHAPTER 10

▼

When Saturday came Tom went down to the quay to meet any visitors from St Mary's who might be coming to the talk. But there were no new arrivals on the late morning boat or the next one.

Leyne was pacing impatiently up and down in the yard as Gray took the tractor down to await the arrival of the freight boat which he expected would have a delivery of fodder for him.

He was just loading up and waving the freighter off when he noticed a smart little craft pull into the bay. He stopped to watch as an older man and young girl got into the dinghy. The man rowed over to the slipway used for launching the island's gig and, jumping out into the shallows, helped the girl out and together they pulled the dinghy up onto the slope.

Gray finished loading the trailer and started the tractor up, hoping to catch a closer glimpse of the newcomers. He saw them walking ahead as he was chugging past the pub. The man was leaning on the girl's arm. Even from that distance Gray could tell he was a much older man, possibly the girl's father or grandfather. The man hailed him just as Gray was about to pass them.

"We're hoping we're not too late for the talk in the church hall. Could you direct us?"

Gray noticed the man had a sparse grey beard and salt and pepper moustache. And despite the casual sweater and seaman's cap, something about the clipped precision of his words led Gray to guess he was a vicar or a teacher.

"I'm going that way … it's my aunt who's giving the talk." He hesitated. "If you'd like a lift?" For someone who always shied away from intimacy with others he was suddenly amazed at the ease with which he said that. "It's a bit smelly, I've a load of fodder on board."

"Well, we're not dressed for a tea party as you can see. If you can give me a hand up, Julie'll not mind climbing onto the trailer, will you?"

Gray, gawping at the slim girl whose brown eyes twinkled up at him under a straggle of long dark hair, almost forgot to close his mouth until she said, "Hi! I'm Julie and this is my grandfather."

"Oh! Right. Hop on then."

When they arrived at the church hall Gray saw his aunt waiting by the open door looking flustered and anxiously glancing up and down the coastal path. His passenger jumped down from the tractor with considerable alacrity considering he must be at least sixty, thought Gray. He held out his hand to Leyne.

"I'm James Jenner, ex-chaplain to the Isles and you must be Miss Golighy. I've read about your interest in ancient and mediaeval history."

"Oh?" she replied.

"A friend of mine in Edinburgh sent me an article about the archaeological society he belongs to up there. Your name was mentioned."

Gray, watching her closely, could have sworn she almost blushed but it was hard to tell since the day was hot and he guessed she was in quite a sweat.

"And this," he said as Julie joined him, wiping down the seat of her jeans, "is my granddaughter, Julie."

"I'm afraid I won't be giving a talk today after all. No one has turned up and it's way after three now. And I somehow don't think anyone from the island is coming." She closed the door behind her. "Why don't you both come up to the farm and we can have an informal discussion."

"Fine by me. I'd like that," said the chaplain. "The history of these islands has long intrigued me. Perhaps you'll be able to answer some of my questions about runic inscriptions and why there are so many barrows on such a small island. But I guess Julie won't want to come." He looked at her enquiringly.

"Sorry grandpa."

"I think she'd prefer just to walk and look round the island … perhaps your nephew …?" He looked at Gray encouragingly.

Gray reddened.

"Good. Of course he'll show her the island. Gary, take the tractor back and get unloaded." Leyne spoke in a voice that brooked no refusal. "Come along vicar, let's walk. It isn't far."

"Mind, Julie, not too long. We need to sail before it gets dark."

Soon Leyne and the vicar were walking off and chatting away like old friends.

"She isn't half bossy," said Julie. "So, you're Gary?"

"No. Gray." He looked embarrassed. "That's what I prefer to be called."

"Well Gray, we'd better get your tractor dumped first." She climbed up beside him.

"Where'd you like to go?" he asked shyly.

"Wherever you like," she said, glancing up at him under her long dark lashes.

He was silent as they drove back to the farm thinking furiously how he could find enough on St Hellicks to interest such a gorgeous girl, or any girl for that matter. He'd never had anything to do with girls. He could take her to see the Old Man of Gugh, a huge standing stone, or menhir. But would she like such things?

"Would you like to see seals, or the special places?" he asked as they set off to walk across the Downs.

"Special? Meaning what? If you mean historic things you can forget it. I'm not into old ruins."

"Seals then?"

"If you insist," she said looking bored.

This was not going to be easy. Maybe the seals wouldn't show if he had someone with him. They always came when he went down to the shore and called to them. He'd never doubted his ability to call them, but now ... he felt strangely nervous, unsure of himself.

As they approached St Warna's bay the girl was chattering brightly about staying on St Mary's with her grandpa during the holidays. Why holidays, he wondered? Surely schools would have started on the mainland by now.

"When will you be going back to school?" he asked.

"School?" she snorted, convulsing with laughter. "You thought I was still at school? No way. I'm taking a break from all that, although Mum's pestering me to go on to college to take my exams."

His heart sank unaccountably. That would make her at least a year his senior. But maybe not. Perhaps it was just that she was so … what was the word? Sophisticated?

He beckoned her to climb down to where a gritty sprawl of gravel and sand nudged between flat rocks and placed his finger on his lips.

"I'm going to call them but we'll have to be very quiet and keep still," he said

"Huh! How can you call if you keep quiet?"

He felt she was mocking him. How could he explain that when he concentrated he could taste their saltiness, smell their oily bodies, hear the chunk, chunking noises they made to each other, feel their sleek passage through the waves. And yes, he could soundlessly call them in the depth of his thoughts.

"Well?" She was looking bored again and began to turn to go.

"No, wait," he placed his hand on her arm. "Now, now, I can sense them."

"Sense them!" she spluttered incredulously.

"Watch! Look!" he pointed to beyond the edge of the bay. "Out there! Here they come." Three round greyish black heads, like three curious dogs, popped up through the translucent green water, round black shining eyes gazed at the pair. There they remained, motionless, except for their quivering muzzles.

"Ooh!" squealed Julie. "Wow … I really didn't believe …"

At that moment the sea rippled and all that remained were three swirling circles on the surface of the sea.

"Oh! They've gone."

"No, they'll follow us as we walk across to the other side of the island. Keep looking and you'll see them coming up for air from time to time but they'll be following us." Yet Gray was puzzled. Usually they would come up onto the flat rocks and stay a while when he called them. It was quite out of character and disappointing. He'd wanted to show off in front of Julie.

"So you really did call them and they came," she said, coming level with him as he was pushing through the thick high bracken growing across the path. "Are you some sort of freaky guy?"

The word really hurt. He wished he'd never agreed to show her the island. Why did people always think he was a freak? He remembered wondering why no one else seemed to be able to hear the pulsating of the tusk. Did that really make him weird? Julie clearly thought being able to communicate with the seals was odd. For him it was such a natural thing to do. Why did she think it was so strange?

"Well?"

He remained silent.

"Oh come on. Sorry I said freak. But it was kind of weird. How did you just do that?"

"I've never really thought about it. I've always been able to speak to them as a child. But something happened recently that's changing things on the island and I didn't know whether I would be able to call them today."

"Oooh! Do tell!"

"Perhaps. Later on," he said, wishing he'd held his tongue. If he told her about the tusk he was sure she'd only scoff. "Would you like to go over to Gugh? The tide's out and we could get over and back before it turns."

"Gugh?"

"Yes, it's over to the east. No one lives there. It's a really wild place just connected to Hellick's with a sand bar."

"If there's time. Is it far?"

"No. The island is so small you could walk right round it in an hour."

"Well, I do have to get back before dark. We could get cut off or something and then ..." She didn't finish her sentence because he'd stopped dead in front of her.

"What is it?"

"Sh!" He turned to her and, whispering, said, "We'll go back another way."

"Why? What's wrong?"

"Come on, let's go," he urged.

But it was too late. Emerging from the bracken were two figures, Jo Henderson and Rod Treverick.

"Hey, there Loony!" called Jo. "Got yeself a girlfriend?"

"My!" whistled Rod. "Ain't she something!"

"Keep going, Julie," said Gray grimly.

"Oh, ho! Keep going, Julie," Jo mimicked. "Ain't ye coming out wi' me Julie?"

"Get lost," she said. "I could eat you lot for supper." She placed a hand on her hip and swaggered past with the exaggerated pose of a model on a catwalk.

"Whoo hoo!" breathed Rod, all round eyed. "She's a model, like on telly."

"Of course," she said derisively.

Gray took hold of her other hand and urged her towards the path leading down to the sand bar. But shaking him off she scampered along the path towards the shore. When he caught up with her she had thrown herself down on the sand and was breathless with laughter.

She looked up at him. "Why do they call you Loony?"

"Because I never went to school."

"What? Never?"

"No. Dad used to be a teacher and when he settled here he chose to educate us himself."

"That accounts for it then, all that time on your own, all that staring at the sea on your own."

He frowned.

"Sorry, I don't mean you're really loony, not like that ignorant lot said. It's something to do with photons."

Gray frowned even more.

"I remember reading once about a girl who lived in a small village near the sea in Brittany, oh, ages ago. She spent hours gazing at the sea and became famous for her telepathic powers. It was said it was caused by the hypnotic effect of the millions of sparkling light photons bouncing off the water."

She got up, stretched, and linked her arm through his. "Say, I really like you Gray. You're different."

He smiled.

Perhaps he would take her to have a chat with his friend, the Old Man of Gugh, after all.

CHAPTER 11

▼

"In my book," said Julie as they trudged back to Shearwater farm, "anyone who can call up seals without opening his mouth and who can communicate with a mouldy piece of stone is bloody marvellous, not loony. Did it really speak to you?"

Gray only smiled.

"But you still haven't told me about that recent happening that you say has changed things. How? Come on, you can tell me."

"Well," he hesitated, "I told you I've always been able to sense when the seals were around, but as for the Old Man of Gugh … maybe I did make it up, perhaps I didn't really hear anything."

"No, you're kidding. You heard alright, because how else did you know the tide had already turned? Good grief! We were only just in time. Another second and we'd have been cut off."

"Instinct, that's all."

"Wish I'd got half your instinct then. Are you going to spill or not?"

They had reached the top of the hill overlooking Periglis bay and someone years ago had thoughtfully put an old bench there.

Julie sat down and kicked off her trainers. Nice feet, he mused, fancifully imagining them slipping into a pair of his softest handmade leather sandals.

"Spill?" Gray was not sure what she meant.

"Yes, about the *happening.*"

"It was something I found on the shore, a kind of whale's tusk, not a happening really. It makes sounds that no-one seems to be able to hear except me and ... my aunt's cat."

"Is that all? Nothing too weird about that. You do seem to have extraordinarily keen senses."

"But what if ..." he paused. Could he really say this to a girl he'd only met a few hours ago when he daren't say it even to himself? He began again: "What if it somehow had caused me to have extraordinary powers ... like supernatural powers?"

"You should be so lucky."

"Oh, so you think that's alright then? It wouldn't freak you out?"

"Depends. If it was seeing the answers to my exam questions, no, not the tiniest bit." She laughed. "Don't look so serious. Nobody's got that kind of power."

"But I cured one of our cows just by putting my hand on her when she was very sick."

"That's awesome," said Julie. "But why did you say this object ... er, tusk, or whatever it is, has caused everything to change?"

"I can't explain yet. All I know is that everything's different."

"And the tusk?"

"I can show you, if you like."

She looked at him. "Okay by me. Don't think I don't believe you, you've already surprised me rigid. But maybe you're taking things far too seriously. You ought to have more fun. Why not come over to visit us next week?"

Gray opened his mouth to reply but couldn't find the words. She couldn't be serious.

"Grief! Is that the time?" she said glancing at her wristwatch. "I should be getting back. Race you to the farm." She streaked off barefooted across the field, trainers in hand.

Gray caught up with her.

She was sitting on a furrow at the edge of the potato field nursing her ankle. "Serves me right for not stopping to put my trainers on. Come on then! Where's this magic talisman? Can't wait to see it."

They were crossing the yard when Julie's grandfather called to them from the door of the farmhouse.

"Where do you think you're going? It's already getting dusk and we must be on our way before dark. Thanks for the tea and discussion," he said, turning to Leyne who was standing beside him. "Now we really must go. Julie!" he called again, as neither she nor Gray seemed inclined to stop.

"But Grandpa, we were going to see the cows."

"Another time."

"Gary will run you down to the quay in the tractor," said Leyne.

Gray shrugged, suddenly regretting taking Julie into his confidence. He went off to fetch the tractor, almost relieved that they had been prevented from visiting the barn.

"Well, goodbye and thanks for the discussion," said James to Leyne as he clambered up into the cab beside Gray. "I've always wanted to believe that St Hellicks was the fabled Casseritides, the Roman tin island."

"Of course we'll need more factual proof than just the bits that I've been able to dig up," said Leyne.

"Yes, indeed, more factual proof," said James without conviction. "Still, it was a very interesting hypothesis you put forward."

"Quite an informative afternoon," said James to Gray as they chugged down to the quay.

"I would have thought you'd have had the advantage of my aunt having lived out here longer," said Gray, genuinely surprised that a man of his background didn't already know all there was to be known about the history of the islands. It seemed odd him asking about barrows and ancient inscriptions—what had he called them? Runic, or something like that?

James cast Gray a strange look and then, as if surprised by the query, covered it with a sort of false smile. "Hmm. She understands a great deal about the historical background."

"What did you mean about the tin island?"

"She's sure the Romans came to these islands, or what was then called the Casseritides, looking for tin. Perhaps they did come. After all, I believe they later renamed the islands Sculla or Sillena, not sure which, after one of their goddesses. But she doesn't begin to understand the legends, nor what motivates the people here. Not her territory, I fear. Interesting!" he pouted, "but it wasn't quite what I was looking for."

He sat musing a while until Gray picked up the courage to ask what he had been expecting.

"I'm afraid I didn't come clean with your aunt. You see, I'm a member of SIPP," he said.

"Sorry?"

"SIPP," he smiled. "It stands for Society for the Investigation into Paranormal Phenomena. It may seem odd that an ex-vicar should be interested in such matters. But when I saw the word Casseritides I was convinced your aunt might be on to something. There are some weird legends around that name."

"What do you mean?"

"Oh, there are all sorts of stories about the drowned landscape and wandering ghosts. And, there have been some pretty disturbing things going on round here for some months now."

"Like?" Gray tightened his grip on the steering wheel.

"Like the strange behaviour of birds. You must have noticed. We would expect to see migrants at this time of year, yet they're all giving St Hellick's a wide berth. And then, there seems to be some kind of magnetic force west of Hellick's that's disturbing fish and shipping … there was the disappearance of a fishing boat … Oh!" he paused and looked at Gray aghast. "I'm most terribly sorry. I … I didn't realise, about your father. I mean, it wasn't until your aunt told me …" His voice trailed off as though embarrassed.

Gray pulled on the brake and stopped the tractor suddenly. What did this stranger know?

"I'm really sorry. For one of my calling that was blessed tactless of me," continued the vicar.

Gray remained very quiet, not knowing how to prevent the turmoil of emotion welling up inside him, not understanding his reactions or how to deal with them. He'd never come this close to being so overwhelmed with feeling in someone else's company. Was it anger, grief? He couldn't place it.

Julie was shouting up to them. "Hey, what's going on?"

"Only me," James shouted back. "It was my fault. I was asking Gary to identify a bird."

Gray wondered whether vicars were excused from telling the truth.

"Look, we'll get to the bottom of it," he said as Gray started up again "Whatever's happening, there has to be a cause."

Neither spoke again until they reached the gig boathouse.

"Well, here we are! Thanks again."

"I'll help you haul off," said Gray.

"I'd appreciate that," said James as he carefully steadied himself down the steep slipway.

"You didn't tell me what your grandfather was really after," whispered Gray to Julie. "Look, keep it to yourself what I told you."

"Okay. Can't talk now. Give me a call." She took a notepad out of her jeans' pocket and scribbled down a number.

Gray stuffed the piece of paper under his belt and after he'd helped them to launch the dinghy watched as they pulled away from the shore. Julie waved as they reached the boat and he waited until they sailed out of the Sound before returning to the farm.

He still wasn't sure why he'd asked Julie to keep his secret. Admittedly he hadn't liked the way her grandfather was snooping around but perhaps that wasn't the real reason. He'd never spent a whole afternoon in any girl's company before, let alone shared a secret with her and the thought gave him a warm feeling.

It had been an unusual day. Would he ever see her again? Her grandfather had said something puzzling about a magnetic force disturbing shipping to the west of Hellick's. Maybe he could find out more from Tom. Then perhaps that would be reason enough for him to go over on a visit. Or ...? His mind raced on. Was it possible?

He drove back to the potato field in a frenzy. What if someone else had passed that way? He stopped the tractor and jumping out searched along the muddy ruts. And still there in the wet earth, just where she'd stopped, were a pair of clearly etched footprints, hers. He traced the imprint with his forefinger recalling her small delicate feet. With the stub of a pencil and a sheet of brown paper ripped from an old bag of potatoes he carefully traced the outline of the prints.

Gray hadn't entered Dad's shed since the fateful day of the great storm but now he knew it was going to be alright to go back there. He pushed open the farm gate. He was going to find a roll of the finest doeskin. He was no longer afraid that his hand would waver. He was going to cut out, in sure clean curves, the most perfect pair of soft white sandals ever made.

His new found joy was harshly broken into by the appearance of his aunt running towards him. She was flailing a bandaged wrist as though in pain.

"Get the doctor quickly," she said in anguished tones. "I can't believe it. I simply can't believe it. Co'burn has gone stark raving mad."

She didn't need to say more. Gray could see the blood seeping through the white handkerchief wrapped around her hand.

"There isn't a doctor on the island, only Jed Rowe the vet."

"A vet!" she spluttered.

"Jed's the best you can get. I'll get him on his mobile. He could be out on his rounds."

Fortunately for Leyne, Jed had just finished a call at Higher Farm and arrived within minutes.

"A cat's bite is worser'n a dog's, worser'n any other pet's," said Jed after injecting Leyne and re-bandaging the arm. "Where's the animal now?"

"He shot off like a wild thing. He's been behaving strange for days."

"Well, when he returns I'll need to look him over. He's not the only creature that's acting odd. The fishermen are complaining about the fish threshing about. Higher Farm are having trouble wi' their cattle and Tom Jenkins tells me one of yer cows was poorly."

"Why wasn't I told, Gary?" said Leyne in an accusing tone.

"Because she's quite well now. Ask Tom."

"I'll take a look anyways while I'm here," said Jed. "Ye can't be too careful. On a small island like this any sickness can spread like wildfire."

"Look if you like. As long as there's no charge," said Leyne. Gray grimaced at her ingratitude. "I'll be selling them anyway."

"Ye'll not be selling anything if yer herd's got the same trouble as the other farm. And my advice to you, missus, is to take a sedative and get some rest. We'll not be knowing how ye'll be ye'self until I've seen that cat."

As Leyne went indoors Jed put his hand on Gray's shoulder.

"Let's look at yer herd then, lad. Something's happening that I don't rightly understand."

CHAPTER 12

▼

That night Gray found it impossible to get to sleep. When, in the early hours of the morning, he finally drifted off, he dreamt of a dark shrouded creature uttering wild, incomprehensible shrieks. He saw a ghostly menhir rising up stone by stone on the shore at Periglis and a line of vivid light running from it to the Old Man menhir on Gugh. It became a circle of light bouncing off the highest points of each of the other off-islands. Then it changed into a burning arrow and sped on to a rock pinnacle out at sea. On, on, it shot, in an easterly direction until it reached the mainland where it burst into flame. A massive sea eagle descended which lunged and tore at his flesh with its powerful beak. With his bare hands he tried to wrench it away and as he flung it against the window he heard the bright snapping and shattering of glass and a screech of unearthly malevolence as the thing plunged to its death.

He awoke in pitch darkness, his pulse racing, his brow streaked with sweat. He sensed he was not alone. Something, a dark wetness, hovered over him. He lay in bed, listening, trying to steady his heart. He could taste salt, not the fresh fishy salt of the seals but a burning choking salt of the drowned.

'Casseritides' … the word came involuntarily to mind. He wanted to cry out but could not. The wet horror crept closer; he jerked up, trembling, leapt out of bed and flung open the door. A black shape streaked out. There was a clatter of falling objects, a window banging and flapping in the night breeze, then all was still.

He waited, half expecting his aunt to have been disturbed by the noise but as she did not appear he closed the door, got back into bed and pulled the bedclothes over his head.

Morning brought rare bright weather. October mornings on the island were so often cloaked in mist but today the sun was blazing through the curtains.

Gray stirred and then jolted up, alert, remembering the terror of his dream. He rushed to open his curtains and was relieved to find that the pane was not shattered. He flung open his door. An overturned vase lay on its side on the landing as though knocked over by someone's or something's headlong flight. The window on the landing was open, just wide enough for a cat to get through … or, the thought appalled him, something insubstantial, the *Rentemen*, or *The Drowned Folk* as they were called by the islanders.

He dressed hurriedly and went down to the kitchen expecting to see his aunt, but she wasn't there; neither was Co'burn.

As he poured himself a glass of milk he caught sight of his reflection in the glass-fronted cupboard. He thought his face looked pinched. Aunt Aleyne's cooking no doubt, or lack of. Still, his body was lean and hard from swimming in the icy cold waters of the bay and he was broad shouldered enough to take part in the eight man gig, not that anyone would ever think to choose an Edmond, he reflected ruefully.

After he'd breakfasted on a shop-bought loaf there was still no sign of his aunt. It struck him that it was Tom's last day and he'd made no mention of whether it was Gray's turn to see to the cows. He ran over to the barn and pushed open the door. The herd had gone. Jed had pronounced them healthy enough so he guessed Tom must have taken them up to the top field. The milking machine had been neatly stacked and everything left tidy.

Gray climbed up into the hayloft and, pulling the hay apart, studied the markings on the tusk with renewed curiosity since Julie's grandfather had spoken about his interest in runic inscriptions. He wondered if that's what these were. Agnes had said such markings might have been made by ancient Icelanders. He traced the outline of the markings with his forefinger and then, holding up his hand, tried to memorise them. As he did, the air seemed to grow thicker around the symbols and then a tingling sensation ran down his finger into his arm and along his spine. He retraced the markings, one by one, memorising them. And as he continued drawing them in the air from memory he became aware that he could touch them. It was as though they were growing solid by the second. One felt spongy and another like fine netting. They began to take on a vibrancy that he could almost see—they were taking shape before his eyes. A sudden tremendous surge of power like a hard punch in the midriff winded him, and a great spinning energy poured into his legs. The air around him grew lighter. He felt a sense of weightlessness as though he was floating in a different element. It lasted only seconds, but afterwards as he pulled the hay back over the tusk Gray experienced a sense of joy so intense he thought he must have broken through into another world. Still vibrating with powerful energy from head to toe he climbed down into the barn below. Afterwards, when he searched for a word to describe the experience of that moment, the only word he could find was 'Shamrocked.'

Once, Dad had taken him and Rob to a fair on the mainland. Gray had never forgotten the incredible feeling of being rotated 360 degrees in a cage called 'The Shamrock'. For both boys the word had stuck and had epitomised the height of exhilaration.

The sensation of power remained. It was a feeling of being able to do anything, achieve anything. He was going to make the sandals for Julie and he was going to make them now.

Gray took Dad's key from a shelf in the barn but when he opened the shed door he took a deep breath as though he was entering a holy place. Everything reminded him of Dad. His tools were there just as he had left them and his coffee mug, the one Rob had bought him from the pottery on St Mary's, stood on the workbench next to a book labelled 'orders'.

He sat down at Dad's bench inhaling the resin, the beeswax, the familiar smell of leather. He reached for the rolls of leather and among them were deep blues, browns, silver even, and white. But white was all he needed. He caressed the soft white doeskin and began to cut, to shape, to sew. And as he worked, he glanced out from time to time through the small window that looked out across the Downs. He remembered the stories about the *Rentemen*, the cursed Drowned Folk who never found rest but roamed among the living ever looking for safe harbourage.

Dad had never held with such stories and at that moment he felt that Rob and Dad were not wandering among such pitiful lost ghouls but were somewhere safe. Time passed as though he was in a dream and he was still hard at work when he heard someone come in through the open door. Gray looked up and saw it was Tom. His face looked haggard and drawn and Gray knew why, as though he had read his thoughts.

"You've had to sell the herd."

"Ay, 'tis a sad day, I'll miss them real bad I will. But, eh?" Tom shook his head in disbelief. "'ow did ye know what I was going to say? 'Twas only done this 'alf hour 'agone. I took the cows up to the field as usual this morning after milking and went back to the cottage. Charlotte and me was thinking what was going to 'appen to us when I stopped work and then there was Jed Rowe knocking at my door and saying as 'ow yer aunt wanted to sell the 'erd and if they was still for sale 'e was interested."

Gray put the half finished sandals down on the workbench. "He said they were healthy but I'm surprised after the scare at Higher Farm."

"Said as he didn't 'ave fears of any sickness 'cos they'd always grazed separate, at the farthest end of the island."

"So you've sold them?"

"As good as. Yer aunt was down at our cottage this morning. I said about the offer and she sort of nodded. But I couldn't make any sense of what she was saying. She looked sorta wild, 'er clothes all undone and kept on about that dratted cat. But it beats me 'ow ye knew?"

"Just guessed. She said she was going to sell them," said Gray but he was surprised himself. It was as though he'd heard what Tom was thinking in his own head.

"Oh, and about the cat. Yer aunt'd been out searching everywhere for it. It didn't come 'ome last night. My Charlotte, bless 'er, said she could almost feel sorry for 'er being in such a state.

Yer aunt mayn't be kind to folks but she loves that creature. Takes all folks, don't it?"

A deep shudder passed through Gray. So it wasn't the ghost of one of the *Rentemen*, all damp and hovering, who had haunted him last night. He could not dismiss the terrible idea that it was the phantom of a drowned cat.

CHAPTER 13

▼

"Them shoes are a beauty, lad," said Tom, picking the sandals up and stroking the soft leather admiringly. "For someone special, are they?"

Gray blushed deeply.

"Good that yer back at yer work. It'll keep ye busy now we're going away."

"Away, Tom?" Gray's face dropped. "Sorry, I don't understand you."

"Catherine, our daughter what lives in Cornwall, sent us the plane tickets. They arrived in the post by last night's boat. We're to visit 'er a while."

"Oh! Just a visit then?" Gray looked relieved. "But you'll be coming back? You'll be sure to be coming back?"

"I'd like to say yes to that, lad. We have to make plans, me and Charlotte, now there's no job 'ere."

"But there's still work here. And, there's the fishing."

"Nah! Lived all me life on this island but there's no work anymore. No one wants a spare 'andyman. They've all got their own families to look out for 'em and the fishing don't bring in enough. When the café was running I could always catch enough crabs for the lunches even when the lobsters wasn't doing well. But now ..." His voice sounded choked and Gray was too overwhelmed to speak.

"Ye'll not 'ave too much to do now and Jed'll always give ye a 'and with the generator if ye get into trouble. It was more at my urging that Jed took the 'erd, knowing as I was leaving."

"Oh! So you've known for some time you were leaving?" Gray pushed the white sandals away. His shoulders sagged as he leaned forward on the bench.

"Ever since yer aunt came we knew we couldn't stay."

"But you could look after ..."

"What? Look after two pigs and a few chickens? Come on, lad! 'Tisn't reasonable to expect she'd pay me for doing that."

"I'll make her." Gray stood up, determination in his look. "I'll make her."

"It's too late. We're going on Tuesday's flight. We've got to go, to try some other way of making a living. Mebbe get some farm work on the mainland. It's breaking our 'earts to leave but it's not for good."

Tom put an arm round Gray who hugged the old man to disguise his welling tears. "Don't take on so. Things'll work out fine, ye'll see. Ye can have *Sea Rover* while's I'm away. P'raps ye'll 'ave more luck fishing than me of late."

"But I couldn't...."

"Take it. Take it on loan, it'll keep ye busy. There's not enough to make a living but it'll make a change from ye always being 'ere cooped up making shoes. An' if I can give ye some advice it's this, 'umour yer aunt!"

"That's the last thing I'm going to do." And the last thing he expected Tom to suggest. Tom's life was now in shreds because of her.

"'ave it yer way. Ye're going to need each other, lad. Ye can't go on fighting 'er."

It was true Gray never passed her without glowering and she never passed him without scolding. Oh, but he was going to miss Tom sorely.

"Well, I'll be off. Plenty for me to do if Charlotte an' me's going to be ready an' packed by Tuesday. Go on then with ye," said Tom gruffly, trying to hide his emotion. "Go find that cat of 'ers an she'll be putty in yer 'ands. An'mebbe," he smiled, "she'll let ye take us over to St Mary's in *Sea Rover* come Tuesday."

"Just let her try to stop me."

When Tom had gone Gray pulled the white leather sandals towards him and held them tightly. *An mebbe Tom, I* will *get to take Se*a *Rover over to St Mary's. An' then who knows?*

*   *   *   *

Gray had found Co'burn last time on the Downs, but he guessed the cat's instinct would make him too scared to go back there. Perhaps he'd got trapped somewhere between the rocks. There were some deep crevices on Wingletang, if that's where he'd gone.

Gray decided to cross over to Wingletang by the shop and set off along the main path. A buggy passed him as he reached the top of the hill and pulled up. Gray recognised the driver as one of Tom's drinking pals, Bob Stirling.

"Tom Jenkins is leaving come Tuesday, I hear. 'Tis all that fat cow's doing."

Bob had never spoken more than a couple of words to Gray in his life.

"I suppose you mean my aunt?"

"Aye, 'er. She's not welcome on our island."

"It's not your island," said Gray flatly and started to move away.

"Oh, Aye! Ye'll soon find out whose island it is."

Bob started the engine and drove off without giving him another glance.

There was still, Gray knew, an old simmering feeling among the islanders against his Dad and now, against his aunt. He sensed eyes watching him, fixing on his back as he walked on. When he passed a group of women outside the Post office they stopped chatting immediately. He wanted to ask about the cat but he knew they'd just shrug and turn away. And as he rounded the corner into Post office Lane he caught a sniggering remark about 'those Edmonds.'

He made for Cove Vean with his head held high but his face burning with anger. He was half wishing he'd never bothered to look for his aunt's wretched cat, that he'd stayed on his own patch. All of a sudden he saw how Dad, living as a free man, being his own person, living his own truth, had been out of step.

It seemed as if it *did* matter to others in this place that you generated your own electricity, drew your own water, recycled your own rubbish, grazed your own herd separately, produced your own milk, baked your own bread and caught your own fish. It *did* matter that the rest of the island helped each other out, went to the same school, had open grazing, shared their catch and bought produce from the shop.

He hadn't known until now, now he was in danger of losing Tom, how bitter it was to be excluded. Dad had been so strong, he hadn't cared what anyone said and Gray had pretended he didn't care either—but suddenly he couldn't pretend any longer. The loss of the *Minerva* hadn't just taken Dad's life. For a while it had left Gray with a deep loss of his own individuality. While Dad was alive everything had cocooned him in the belief that it was the right way to live. Now he felt he was just bursting out into the fresh air, cold and shivering from beneath a huge waterfall.

When he reached the cove he saw two boys dragging something long, thin and black out of the water and his heart froze.

Gray didn't need to ask what the black shape was. He knew.

He veered off in a westerly direction to avoid returning by the main path and came to the little well which nestled in a hollow at the base of a hill overlooking St Warna's Cove. A mediaeval shrine once stood beside the well and at first he was not surprised to see a wreath of mistletoe lying on the first of the three steps leading down into the stone-chambered well. The islanders even now still held rituals here throwing pins into the well and invoking the saint to bring them 'goodly bounty.' And he knew there were tales of a light being left burning by the well to lure sailors onto the reefs that surrounded the isle. A treacherous bounty indeed! No wonder there were so many *Rentemen*, unhappy ghosts, on the island. But when he looked more closely he was horrified to see that the wreath appeared to have been viciously torn and slashed.

It was then he heard a keening sound, a whining or moaning as if someone was in pain. A shape emerged from the hedge below and he was shocked at the almost unrecognisable figure of his aunt. Her hair, usually scraped back, was flying about wispily and her black shawl trailed behind her in the muddy path. She began calling, at first in a half strangled tone, "Co,

Co, Co'burn" and then again but more shrilly "Co'burn, Co, Co Co'burn."

But there was no answering mewl.

She was heading for the path that led up to the gigantic and strangely named monolith 'The Nag's Head'. Gray followed, feeling all antagonism towards her fading.

Because the boulders and huge granite rocks on this part of the island were worn into such grotesque shapes, Gray, watching them from a distance, often felt they moved. And today as he followed his aunt up the steep bramble-covered slope the irregularly shaped stones that stood in a circle around the base of the Nag appeared to be emerging from the shadow cast by the afternoon sun in a gliding or weaving movement. Gray stood and watched in fascination.

Leyne was now just below the stone circle. She too had paused, no doubt to get her breath. It was no easy climb and he reckoned her weight would have slowed her down, but she was clearly in such a frenzy of passion that she must have pushed herself to her limit.

Then the shadows changed and Gray saw with shock that he'd made a mistake. The stones hadn't shifted. Instead the scene before him filled him with dread. A small group of islanders were gathered in a circle around the base of the monolith and they appeared to be performing some kind of dance. Gray had heard of 'Guise-dancing' from Charlotte but had never seen it before. He supposed it meant 'guise' as in 'disguise' and guessed this might be what it was, some kind of ritual to appease the drowned spirits of islanders lost at sea. The dancers, although it could hardly be called a dance, were wearing black hoods and their faces were concealed in shadow. They were circling the base of the Nag and every few steps threw up their hands in unison almost as though they were moving to a subterranean rhythm for there was no sound except the sighing of the breeze.

His aunt seemed to be either unaware of the seriousness of breaking into this ritual, or so overcome with grief that she took no heed of the threat that seemed to emanate from the very centre of the circle. She advanced into their midst and while Gray couldn't hear what she said, supposed she must have asked if they knew where Co'burn was. Two of the dancers threw off their hoods and moved towards her. He thought he recognised Agnes Treverick and Molly Stokes. As he came closer he saw how heartless their expressions were. Then Agnes Treverick broke into an angry cackle.

"Are you mad? Do you think we're going to go looking for a cat?"

"A cat that's scared all our birds away," cried another.

"Twitchers bring in the money, the money that buys things, woman," said Molly Stokes in a high-pitched voice. "And now there ain't any migrants stopping 'ere because of that cat o' yours. Ye're a curse on this island."

But Leyne had gone beyond reason. "One of you's poisoned him!" she shrieked in frantic tones, turning round at all the faces closing in on her.

"Oh yes, we didn't rest until he was put down," taunted another.

Gray couldn't be sure who was the first to cast a stone in his aunt's direction. A man or maybe a boy, then others began to shower her with small pebbles calling out in loud bullying voices.

Gray felt a burst of energy in his arms and shoulders. Instinctively he moved his hands and began tracing in the air before him the runic symbols he'd seen on the tusk. Once again he felt them becoming tangible and the energy that flowed from them propelled him into the centre of the now angry crowd. Agnes' cackle could be heard above the noise and Jo Henderson's younger brother who was poised to throw the next pebble stood with his arm suspended in mid-air as though paralysed. Gray caught Agnes' eye as he strode into the midst of them and the cackle died in her throat.

He sensed the power in him and the voice that spoke didn't seem to be his own voice. "Are you mad or sick? What kind of sickness is on this island? You're behaving like cattle."

"How dare you, brat! I'm betting it was you as cursed the cattle," yelled Bob Stirling, pointing a stick at Gray and then dropping it as Gray glared at him.

"I knew it was him," shrieked Agnes, now emboldened by Bob's attack. "His dad cursed my lads when they was small. They was bitten all over with strange bites, burning, stinging marks they 'ad, all over them that night yer dad cursed 'em."

"It's you is the mad loony lot, you Edmonds," cried Jeff Sparrow. "You should get outa here."

Gray stood his full height, feeling his power growing. They actually believed the innocent remark his father had once made about the crabs biting them as a punishment for their bad behaviour had been a curse. And now they believed Gray had cursed their cattle and brought the sickness because his own herd was safe and healthy. He felt he could curse them right now and they'd believe anything he said.

"If there's any bewitching it's Agnes Treverick's who's done the cursing," he said, then almost regretted it in an instant. What on earth had made him say that?

Agnes shot him a withering look.

"Control your tongue," said Molly Stokes. "How old are you to be speaking like that? Fifteen?"

"Nearly sixteen. And old enough to know bullying when I see it. My aunt asked you a civil question and you are—how many against one?" His eyes swivelled round judging there were at least seven of them.

As if in response the women and boys began sheepishly to turn and walk away. Only Bob remained and Jeff Sparrow.

"You watch it, young fellow," said Bob, meeting Gray's eyes so that Gray felt the older man's will trying to match him down.

"Edmond," he said finally, "you'll regret saying what you did. It isn't just the Trevericks who might track you down now."

Bob let his stare linger for what seemed like an age and then his gaze wavered as if he sensed the difference in Gray. He strode off with Jeff following.

"Thank you!"

Gray turned, hearing his aunt's voice, suddenly realising she was still there.

"But what did he mean about the Trevericks tracking you down?" she asked.

"Oh," he shrugged, "they've just got it into their heads that I've got something of theirs."

"And have you?"

He shook his head.

"But they'll come back Gary, and in force." She picked up her black shawl and pulled it tightly round her. "You've made some real enemies."

Gray shifted a heap of pebbles with his foot. "They could have killed you with these." He bent down to pick up a pebble but also to hide his hands that were trembling. "Agnes Treverick *is* an old witch and I don't care who hears it. And they *were* bullying you. It had to be said, even if there is a price to be paid for saying it."

CHAPTER 14

▼

That night Gray and Leyne ate supper together for the first time. Gray, reflecting on the advice Tom had given him, thought it had been almost prophetic. Yet it was sad that Co'burn going missing should have been the means of bringing them together. Despite her unhappiness Leyne had made a broth of leeks and potatoes and a kind of shepherd's pie with tinned meat. It wasn't up to Charlotte's standards but Gray, realising he hadn't eaten since breakfast, wolfed everything down with relish. They exchanged very few words during the meal since Leyne kept snivelling into her handkerchief and toying with her food.

Just as she was clearing away Gray heard scuffling outside in the yard and went out to look, ignoring his aunt's cautioning him to stay indoors. As he stood in the doorway silhouetted by the light from the kitchen something wet, heavy and obscene hit him in the face. With a growing sense of horror he looked down and there before him on the doorstep lay the bedraggled body of the pitiful drowned cat and he could not resist crying out.

"Is everything alright?" came Leyne's voice from the kitchen.

"Yes," he lied. "Just some lads playing about. They've gone now." He closed the door behind him and, picking up the little body, gently took it and hid it behind the shed where he intended burying it as soon as his aunt had gone to bed. Better that she never knew.

But despite Gray's good intentions their enemies had deemed otherwise. The next morning the sun picked out the heartless white paint graffiti daubed on the walls of the barn, shed and new flat.

'Death to the cat! Good riddance.'

"They've killed him for sure," said Leyne with a groan when she read the scrawl. "He wouldn't have stayed away so long."

Gray could only stare at the walls in disbelief. This was war.

"That Agnes woman," said Leyne. "You said she was a witch."

"I didn't mean to imply she deals in black magic"

"What did you mean?" Leyne marched up to the flat and glared furiously at the mess of white paint on the door. "How do you account for the satanic rites she and the others were performing by the stones?"

Gray was surprised she'd even noticed. She'd seemed so preoccupied with her own loss.

"That was just an annual ritual."

"Exactly! Black magic."

"I think it's a way of appeasing the spirits of the dead, of those drowned at sea."

Gray was wishing he'd never got involved in this conversation.

"Some kind of guilt they have to work off," she said coldly.

"Guilt? What do you mean, Aunt?"

"I know a thing or two about St.Hellick's you may not know. How the islanders deliberately cause shipwrecks."

"No! No! That was centuries ago. With modern navigation ships couldn't mistake the hidden reefs for land any longer. Those stories are about a time way before Bishop Rock lighthouse was built."

"Their intentions haven't changed. I suppose you wouldn't know about the placing of a mediaeval tribute to their saint of wreckers? Their so-called Saint Warna?"

Gray's mind reeled. He was seeing the slashed mistletoe wreath by the well.

Had his aunt been responsible? Had she deliberately tried to destroy the superstitious tribute to the long gone deity? If so, why?

"And," she continued, "I happen to know they still scavenge for bounty from the sea. Claiming salvage, even if it doesn't involve men's lives anymore. They're still invoking the deity to help them in their nefarious trade of evading the law."

Gray was recalling Tom's accusation of the Trevericks and how they kept clear of the customs people, but it surprised him how she had ferreted out that information on her own.

"A historian's a kind of sleuth, didn't you know boy?" she said, giving answer to his thoughts. "They never give up looking for clues. Just let her or the others dare to threaten me. I will stir such a hornet's nest that will make them sorry they ever meddled with me ..." She sniffed and Gray was astonished to see tears in her eyes. What a contradiction the woman was. "If I find out they've harmed my poor Co'burn I'll report her to the authorities. There are artefacts in that shop of hers that are treasure trove and should rightly belong to ..."

But Gray never knew the rest of her sentence as she stopped mid-flow and he saw she was staring across the yard. He turned to see Tom coming over towards them.

"I don't like to be the bearer of bad news, Miss Golighy," he said in an embarrassed tone. "But yer cat's been found."

"Oh, where?" Her face paled as she looked at Tom. "Where is he?"

"Drowned."

Leyne let out a huge gasp

"In Cove Vean. There was talk in the pub last night about it. Charlotte says she's so sorry and she …"

But Leyne had rushed back to the farmhouse and had slammed the door without waiting to hear what Charlotte had said.

"That's a great pity lad, a great pity."

"But that's not all, Tom. She's threatening to report the Trevericks to the Customs.

Tom shook his head sadly. "Not a good idea lad, not a good idea at all. I came 'ere to say goodbye and to ask about yer taking us over in Sea Rover tomorrow. Guess it ain't a good time."

"You've no need to ask her. I'll be taking you whether she agrees or not, but somehow I think she's on my side at the moment."

Tom smiled. "You've been taking my advice lad? Then I suggest ye talks 'er outa ringing the Customs. Anyways, she don't know that it was Trevericks as drowned the cat."

"She knows alright."

"The whole island'll clam up against 'er. No one on St 'ellick's would ever tell on another body on the island, no matter what they'd done. She'll get short shrift 'ere I can tell ye if she does."

"Too late Tom," said Gray, noticing his aunt standing by the kitchen window with the phone in her hand. "I think she already has."

CHAPTER 15

▼

Tuesday morning saw a huge swell on the sea with waves lashing up beyond the halfway point on Burnt Island Daymark. It was going to be a rough journey.

Since his aunt had kept to her room after hearing the news about Co'burn Gray started to scribble a note to say he was taking Tom and Charlotte to St Mary's, but he hesitated over the spelling of Charlotte, abandoned the idea and wrote simply that he was taking *Tom and Sh. to marys and wold be back late.*

With beating heart he went out to the shed took, the white sandals from a shelf, wrapped them in tissue paper and carefully folded his waterproof jacket round the precious parcel.

He waded into the bay and caught hold of *Minerva's* dinghy, which was being tossed and buffeted by the waves, and rowed out to *Sea Rover.* It was the first time he'd handled her alone although he had been allowed to sail *Minerva* once before with Dad in charge.

The thought of pitting his skill alone against the wildness of the sea gave him a rush of elation. He'd known the stretch between Periglis and Porth Conger like the back of his hand since childhood, but this was different. When he managed to

start her up he was filled with joy and a strange sense of libera-
tion as her prow plunged into the foam and he triumphantly
rounded the bay. It was a joy accentuated by the knowledge that
he'd phoned Julie and had been invited to visit.

On reaching Porth Conger he saw to his amazement that the
whole island seemed to be out in force to say goodbye to Tom
and Charlotte. When he cast the landing rope ashore to secure
the boat a dozen hands were at the ready. Gray searched among
the crowd but could see no sign of the Trevericks.

"We'll miss you," came a voice from the crowd and a babble
of good wishes followed.

"Give our love to Catherine."

"We'll keep an eye on things for ye."

"When are you planning to come back home?"

Tom was going through the motions of trying to answer the
questions that were coming at him from all sides and Charlotte
was looking close to tears.

As Gray helped her aboard he found himself wondering how
he was going to feel when the moment came for him to say his
final goodbye. Perhaps what he really wanted to say would go
unspoken, that he wouldn't know how to put his feelings into
words. He'd never been without Tom and Charlotte ever since
coming to the island as a tiny child. It was going to be tough.

As they cast off, a huge cry went up out of fifty throats, like a
lament. Gray, eyes blinded by the salt spray and his own tears,
set his face with determination towards St Mary's. Tom's strong
hand over his, firmly guided him through the heaving seas.

As they sailed into St Mary's harbour Gray's heart gave a
leap. He'd recognised Julie frantically waving from the top of
the quayside steps, her dark glossy hair flying in the wind. He

suddenly felt conscious of his appearance and wondered whether he should have tied his own unruly hair back.

Julie and James had driven down to meet them and James insisted on taking Tom and Charlotte to the airport. During the entire journey Gray's feelings see-sawed between sorrow and elation. He checked the tears by biting his lips when the time came to wave goodbye to his old friends. He couldn't let Julie see him cry.

She chattered all the way back to James' home without waiting for much response, for which he was thankful as he had no heart for talking. When they arrived Gray saw that the house, Star Castle Lodge, which abutted the castle itself, looked down over the Sound between St Mary's and St Hellick's. How many times had he gazed over that same channel wondering about the distant castle walls, or the Garrison walls, as he knew they were called.

Lunch was a simple meal of salad and cold meat but afterwards when Julie brought in the dessert she placed it on the table with a flourish.

"Made it especially for you," said James, beaming at Julie when she served Gray a helping of his favourite blackberry pie.

"But how did she know …?" began Gray. He was beginning to feel more at ease for the first time that day.

"She's good at ferreting things out is my granddaughter. Don't underestimate this little sleuth."

The word stirred an uncomfortable memory, for that was exactly how Aunt Aleyne had described herself. He wondered how she had reacted to his hastily scribbled note about leaving without saying a word. This was followed by a disturbing image of the Trevericks. Would the Customs have contacted them already?

"You just get her to show you round the castle and the garrison afterwards," continued James, breaking into his thoughts. "Ask her about the Royalists' activities here during the civil war. She's become a real source of information about them and Cromwell since she came to stay."

"A real source of trivia, you mean," she said, playfully tweaking his beard.

"Well, you can see, Gary …," said James

"Oh, Gray, please grandfather."

"Alright then, Gray. You can see we are well placed here, barricaded from invasion by sea, thanks to these old fortifications and incidentally on a direct line with a network of monolithic sites—the no longer extant one at Periglis, The Nag's Head and your Old Man of Gugh."

Gray glanced at Julie. What had she told her grandfather? Was this the right time to speak about his persistent dream of seeing a huge lighted monolith on the shore of Periglis, and of his knowing, since the arrival of the tusk, that something beyond his comprehension was happening on St Hellick's? Somehow Gray detected an air of distance between them as though the older man did not completely approve of him. He pushed his hair off his face self-consciously and wished he'd worn his best sweater instead of his old navy one.

But James was still talking about how those lines of earth energy, ley lines was how he termed them, passed straight through the Star to Bant's Carn on St Mary's. And then on across the sea to Bodmin Moor. Gray registered with surprise that he was saying that all the points were aligned to the midwinter solstice and thus formed part of an ancient ritual landscape.

"There's enough energy still in those old stones of yours on St Hellick's to qualify as trigger points for a vast mysterious power grid."

Gray remembered he'd spoken to him about a mysterious power on the island before. Maybe that was the kind of power that the islanders felt when they banded together to dance and chant like the day he'd come across them dancing around the Nag.

"Do you know anything about 'Guise Dancing'?" Gray found himself asking, more out of wanting to contribute something relevant to the conversation than anything.

"I've read about it. Why do you ask? I wouldn't have thought there'd been any ritual dancing around here like that for hundreds of years."

Gray's stomach churned.

"At least," James continued, "not to my knowledge. The old legends about Casseritides speak of such dances as a means of propitiating pagan gods and goddesses to prevent a return of the great floods and later, as the original meaning became lost, as a way of easing the passing of lost souls at sea."

"Oh, it was just something Charlotte told me about," said Gray, hoping it sounded unimportant. He wasn't sure why he felt so reluctant to discuss his feelings with James. Perhaps because no one had ever taken his premonitions and feelings seriously. That is, not until he'd met Julie. But there was something more. He felt, although he didn't know why, that James was only tolerating him for Julie's sake.

Thinking about The Nag gave him a nasty jar and he was remembering how the Trevericks had been missing from the crowd at Porth Conger.

He caught Julie's eye and saw she was looking at him strangely.

"By the way," he shuffled in his chair trying to appear nonchalant as he spoke, "are the Customs on St Mary's hot in dealing with people who don't declare salvage?"

James looked perplexed by the sudden change of subject. "Salvage? That depends."

"I mean, if it's valuable?"

"All salvage should be reported, unless of course it's something natural like a seal's carcass or such like. Some years ago a German cargo ship, the *Cita,* ran aground off Mary's. Boatloads of folk came from the off-islands and collected trainers, sweaters, shirts, enough to last them a lifetime. Nothing really 'valuable' but, I believe it was all declared and recorded."

"What about undeclared salvage?"

Julie was twirling a lock of hair round her finger, observing first her grandfather and then Gray, just as if she was a spectator watching a game.

"I daresay there are pretty severe penalties. Why do you ask?" James' eyes narrowed as he looked at Gray over his spectacles.

"What if I knew that my aunt had reported that someone on St Hellick's had a store of undeclared treasure trove?"

Julie gave a low whistle of surprise and Gray realised his mistake too late.

"That," said James, tapping his bottom lip, "would be a serious oversight on *someone's* part. I wonder why your aunt would do that?"

"It was during the 'Guise Dancing'," said Gray, realising that by having said too much he would now have to explain. "She accused the Trevericks of killing her cat. They attacked her and so she reported them."

"Guise dancing? Really?" James raised his eyebrows. "In this day and age? Hellick's has always been different, a bit on the wild side and perhaps even lawless, but that is so weird. I, that is, the SIPP really believe something more's happening over there." James shook his head. "Did I tell you that the society's Geiger counters show there is an unusual surge of electromagnetic activity in and around Hellick's?"

Julie leaned forward, a gleam of eagerness in her eyes. She jerked her head towards Gray, as if to say 'go on, tell him about the 'talisman' you found'.

As if sensing the boy's reluctance to say more, James got up from the table and began to clear away the remains of the meal.

Gray's mind was whirling with indecision and doubt. He was so unused to confiding in anyone. He felt trapped, awkward and immature. He should have kept quiet. The knot in his stomach tightened and he felt he was going to be sick. He got up to help but knocked a plate onto the floor in his haste.

"So sorry," he muttered. "Bathroom ... I have to use the bathroom."

"Surely," said James. "Top of the stairs on your left."

"Thanks," said Gray, making an embarrassed and hasty retreat.

On his way back to the dining room the door to the kitchen was open and he distinctly heard James say, "I don't want you getting involved, Julie. I tell you, they're a weird lot on Hellick's, weird and dangerous."

"Not Gray though, grandpa. He's great."

"I just think you should back off. He's led a wild life, acts a bit like a caged animal, and then there's the unsolved mystery about his father, you know."

"Oh, really grandpa! Isn't your psychic society stuff getting to you a bit?"

Gray coughed to let them know he was there. James came out of the kitchen carrying a tea towel.

Gray supposed he should offer to help but he was too angry about being called a wild animal. He stood there without saying a word, just glaring in the direction of the kitchen until James hurried back and picked up a tray saying, "Now I suggest you two go off to explore the castle and let an old man catch up with his rest."

✳   ✳   ✳   ✳

"Why the secrecy?" said Julie as they stood on the battlements of Star Castle overlooking the sea with the sound of the wind and the screeching of gulls in their ears.

"What do you mean?" said Gray in an almost sulky tone.

"Why didn't you spill about that talisman of yours?"

"I've said too much already. And I don't honestly think my 'talisman' as you call it, has anything to do with what your grandfather may think is happening on Hellick's."

Julie pushed her hair out of her face and raised her eyebrows at him. "Then why did you tell me that since finding it everything had changed?"

He shook his head and looked away into the distance, unable to face those penetratingly clear eyes.

"How has everything changed?" she persisted.

"Well," he said, trying to make light of it. "I met you for a start."

"No! Seriously." She punched him playfully.

"I began to see things, to know things, to feel … Oh! it's so difficult to explain." Gray was really struggling. Julie was the last person in the world whose sympathy he needed to lose. At least she didn't appear to hold her grandfather's view of him.

"Go on, try me, I'm a good listener. So long as you keep it simple. And I promise I won't breathe a word to anyone if you don't want me to."

"It's not that," he hesitated. He remembered her calling him freaky when he took her to see the seals.

"Alright, alright," she said as if reading him. "You're not the tiniest bit loony, okay?"

"I think," he began tentatively, "what I've found has a controlling energy. It's as though it has a mind of its own. I feel dead powerful around it and the markings on it seem almost to come alive. I've always been able to know things before they happened but now I'm sure I can tell what people are thinking."

"And what am *I* thinking right now?" She looked up at him.

Gray blushed and looked at his feet.

"Ah!" she smiled. "You're thinking it's too early? That I couldn't have fallen for you so quickly?"

"I … I …" he stammered, since that was exactly what he'd been thinking.

But she bent down and picking some moss from the ancient walls threw it at him and ran off down the granite steps looking back at him over her shoulder, smoothing her hair and laughing in such a way that Gray thought he would never again boast about his telepathic powers.

CHAPTER 16

▼

The sun was just a strip of burnt orange on the horizon and the light was fading as Gray started up *Sea Rover's* engine. As Julie scrambled back up the quayside steps he remembered the gift he had brought her. He could have called her back but was suddenly abashed, not knowing how to give it to her or what to say. Already she was running over to the sea wall so that she could wave to him as the boat ploughed into the waves of the Sound.

It was too late. She wouldn't have liked the sandals anyway. She was too smart, too fashionable to wear homemade sandals. But despite his forgetting this gift and James' comments about him, he still felt buoyed up by the visit and carried Julie's image in his mind all the way back to St Hellick's.

The sky was still slashed orange-red but the outline of the land was now dark with black jagged rocks as he sailed into Periglis Bay. He felt a sense of heaviness and oppression especially as he remembered James' cautionary words as they left the Lodge to go down to the quay: 'The Customs will act on any information given them and they don't like informers any more than any one else. On an island as small as Hellick's this could stir a lot of trouble.'

And that's just what Tom had said, thought Gray, sinking into a reverie as he cast anchor.

*   *   *   *

It was strange how the atmosphere back home felt different from Mary's. There was the same salt tang of the sea but mingled with it were the familiar odours of tar, bruised bladderwrack and samphire, and the herby scent of chamomile and fennel.

He inhaled deeply. Then sniffed the air again. Odd, he thought he smelt smoke. No one burnt rubbish randomly. All household rubbish was burnt in a specially allocated place at a specific time; the rest was transported in huge hempen sacks by sea to a disposal centre on St Mary's. As he climbed up from the bay and passed the church the smell of burning intensified. He sensed danger and began to race towards the farm.

There was a sudden blast from the house. Smoke drifted thickly, blackly enveloping, choking him. He pushed open the farm gate to see flames flashing through the smoke from the kitchen window. The back door was flung open and he felt his heart pound as his aunt stumbled out into the yard with blackened face.

"Gary!" she cried out coughing and spluttering. "Get help, quickly."

But there was no time. Turning on the hosepipe used for sluicing down the farmyard, he directed the full jet through the smashed, blackened kitchen window frame. Then wordlessly handing the hose to his aunt, he dragged the water butt from beside the shed, snatched the pipe from her and pushed a bucket into her hand.

At length the fire was under control as black rivulets of water hissed and steamed through door and window into the yard.

"That witch's brood, young devils," breathed Leyne, "could have burnt me alive."

Gray, knowing exactly who she meant, turned abruptly, as if to chase down to the main quay after them. But Leyne put out a restraining hand.

"No, don't. They'll be home and safe by now and it wouldn't help."

"But I can't let them get away with it. Look at you, look at the mess," he said, going into the smouldering kitchen, his sandals squelching on the soggy smoke encrusted carpet. "How did it happen? Did you see them?"

"I was in the back room when I heard the door open so I came through thinking it must be you." She stopped, panting for breath. "There were three of them, all Trevericks. I saw them clearly, they knew I'd seen them. They shouted some filth at me, then something about my reporting them. One of them came up from behind the others and threw a lighted rag into the kitchen. Everything caught so quickly."

"Petrol," said Gray. "That's why. They'd have soaked it in petrol."

"I just couldn't think. I had to get out."

"You're not hurt?"

She looked surprised at the question. Gray was surprised himself. It seemed such a short while ago they had been at each other's throats.

"I might have guessed what would happen," Gray sighed. "I'm sorry I didn't call you before I went out. I left you a note."

"I heard you go out and came down just after you'd left and saw it."

Gray was still wondering how the Trevericks could have known they'd been reported so soon, when Leyne said, "The customs boat anchored in Periglis shortly after midday."

"Hmm! James said they wouldn't waste time?"

"Who?"

Ignoring the question, Gray pressed on with his own concerns. "So they came up here to the farm?"

"Yes," Leyne coughed and wiped black phlegm from her mouth. "They interrogated me ... wanted me to sign forms. As if *I* would sign their papers. Treated me as if I was some sort of criminal."

In their eyes, you are, thought Gray, remembering what James had said about the attitude on the islands to informers. The customs officers must have gone straight on to Agnes' shop and of course she would have been completely unprepared. So this was their revenge and the hatred that had been simmering against the Edmonds for years had erupted in this vicious attack.

"I'll have to leave, Gary," Leyne said unexpectedly, banging her fist on the wall as if giving vent to repressed fear and anger. "I can't stay here. I'll go to stay with my friend in Penzance. You should come too. You've nothing to keep you here."

"This is my home. Do you think a bunch of creeps like the Trevericks are going to drive me away after what they've done tonight?"

"But that won't be the end of it. You'll be in real danger if you stay and you know it. And it isn't just the Trevericks I'm thinking about." She lowered her voice. "There's something more, something that almost stopped me coming out here in the first place." She grabbed hold of his wrist, turning him towards her. Her grasp was strong and powerful. Her eyes became steely and fierce.

Gray was startled by the sudden change in her. The power of her fear ran through him like an electric shock.

"I was given a warning."

"A warning? When?"

"Before I came here. A voice, a terrible choking voice as though that of some drowning creature warned me to stay away. It was the way it said the name *Casseritides,* as though something cataclysmic was going to happen."

Gray pulled away from her. "Those are just the old Casseritides legends about the seas rising and wiping out the land," he said controlling the tremor in his voice. He felt icy cold. "These islands have been eaten away by the sea for thousands of years. There's more land under the sea round here than above it. They even say we were once attached to the mainland. They're just stories, aunt."

"Maybe!" Her shoulders suddenly sagged and she sighed as though she'd allowed her weakness and fear to show and to reveal the frightened woman beneath the bluster. "Still, you oughtn't to stay. You could get a job or go on to college. You can't say you've got much learning behind you, looking at your spelling."

Gray fell silent. She'd never understand him. How could he explain he was dyslexic? What would be the point even in trying? Yes, Aunt Aleyne had changed for sure over the past few days but they were still miles apart. There was certainly not enough understanding between them for him to consider packing up and going to stay with her for any length of time. He supposed she could still qualify as his guardian even at a distance. And there was Julie. He couldn't leave now even if he wanted to, even if the Trevericks threatened him with the worst thing he could imagine.

"I think we should clean up, and then I'd like to wash and make something to eat, or at least to drink. I've a throat like a tinder box," said Leyne. "The food in the cupboard is probably covered in soot but I might be able to salvage something. Or you could go and dig up a few fresh vegetables."

"I'm not feeling particularly hungry aunt, but you go and wash if you like. I'll clean up the mess and make a hot drink."

"I'll go and just pack a few things then," she said, going to the foot of the stairs. "I'm sorry, Gary, but I don't feel like spending another night in this hostile place."

"The last boat's gone ages ago … unless."

"Yes? Unless?"

Was she really asking him to take her to Mary's now, tonight?

"I've already tied the boat up. You could go first thing in the morning. But if you've decided." He paused, not sure of the wisdom of setting out now. It seemed cowardly to retreat under cover of darkness. It would look like the Trevericks had scored.

"If that's what you really want," he said, hoping his voice didn't betray his anxiety. How was she to know he'd never sailed across the Sound after dark and in addition, there was still a high wind and a strong swell.

"I've already decided. I'm not staying here another night. There's not a single policeman within miles and with that bunch of fanatics on the loose we could be murdered in our beds." She gave a shudder and Gray, who had once thought she was made of steel, saw something almost like terror in her eyes. "Generations of those Trevericks have run wild here for centuries and I guess have been pirates for just as long. It's a wonder they've never been caught before now."

"Most probably they have, over and over again," said Gray, thinking about all the headstones in the churchyard bearing the name of Treverick. Oh, there were also the Jenkins and the Rowes, the good among the bad, but who knew if the good or the bad had held sway all those years ago when life was so hard, so very hard.

"If you can take me tonight I'll stay in a hotel on Mary's and get the passenger boat to the mainland tomorrow," said Leyne abruptly. "What's the name of that hotel on the quay?"

"The Mermaid."

"Good! I'll ring them."

Gray found himself trembling as he tried not to think of coming back afterwards to the empty house, tried not to think of the simmering hostility awaiting him. And while not regretting his aunt's decision to leave he couldn't help feeling that his whole world was falling apart.

And then he remembered Julie and stopped shaking.

*   *   *   *

Before setting out Gray decided to take the precaution of boarding up the kitchen window with slats of wood from the barn. The moon was full and high despite the strong wind making the clouds scurry across it from time to time, so there was no need to use a torch to cross the yard. He could hear the pigs snuffling in the pigpen, as if still alarmed. In the hen house the hens were clucking and flapping around and he could see a silvery trail leading to the barn that confirmed his suspicion that the Trevericks had used petrol. They were going to pay for this.

Storming into the barn, still muttering about revenge, he failed to notice the door was unlocked. But when he climbed up into the loft to search out some suitable lengths of wood he was shocked into silence as he rummaged around to discover that the tusk was no longer where he'd left it.

CHAPTER 17

▼

How could he have been so careless, leaving the barn unfas-
tened! He'd been full of excitement about going to St Mary's,
but that was no excuse. It was irresponsible. Gray fumed at his
own stupidity.

As he returned to the house he was vaguely conscious of his
aunt's huge figure wrapped in her black cape standing in the
doorway, but he was so distracted by the thought of the missing
tusk that nothing registered except the blackness of her shape.

"Well!" she said impatiently.

Then everything came back into focus, her tight lipped nervous expression, her flabby jowls, her scraped back hair.

"I'm ready Gary. I'm waiting."

Gray sensed her edginess, her fear, her wanting to go, to get
it over with and it made him uneasy.

"I need to secure these slats before we leave." He pushed by
her into the kitchen. "Is that all you're taking?" He eyed the
small canvas holdall she was clutching fiercely to her.

"You can send my books and other things on later. If you're
sure you're not coming over to the mainland with me."

"Yes, I'm sure aunt," he said, finishing nailing the last of the slats to the charred window frame.

"Then let's go."

But he wasn't listening to her anymore. A sound, a throbbing, like blood beating in his head, was taking over his whole body, pounding, deafening. Couldn't she hear it? His heart skipped a beat. It had to mean that the tusk was near, didn't it? Yet he remembered how he'd picked up the throbbing the day he rescued Co'burn and then he'd been some distance away. But at least it might still be on the island.

He shook himself, as if shaking would stop the vibration. Leyne was looking at him anxiously.

"We should be going," she said.

Gray wanted to be alone to puzzle out his thoughts, to try to locate the throbbing, but she was right—they ought to go now before it got any later and, listening to the wind getting up and beginning to howl, there could be a storm on the way. He needed to give his whole attention to the journey ahead; there would be time to think about the tusk later.

"I'll go ahead and bring *Sea Rover* in, she's anchored out in the bay. Wait for me on the old quay, aunt. You should be alright to see your way clearly while the moon's still around and with the light from Bishop."

That was true enough. It was almost like daylight as every few seconds the beam from Bishop Rock lighthouse sliced across the track down to the bay.

Getting Leyne aboard was no easy task and despite all Gray's efforts to assist her the boat rocked dangerously as she struggled and panted stepping over the gunwale. But once under way, all fear left him as he felt the boat responding and he pitted his strength against the swell. This was what he was born to do. He felt liberated, free and now the throbbing in his head lessened, giving him time to concentrate on the outline of the coast. How strangely different it looked at night; the familiar rocks and boulders mere shadows, the little coves and inlets so blackly etched. The going was rough but it felt good. In twenty minutes or less he'd be in sight of St Mary's.

As they rounded the last tip of Hellick's the throbbing in his head began to increase alarmingly. The rain had begun and was lashing the windows of the cabin. Dark clouds skimmed across the moon. He felt dizzy, as though he was going to retch, and knew this was not the moment to do so. He had to stay in control. The steering seemed to have a mind of its own; something heavy was forcing the boat landwards. It was being pulled towards the rock that everyone called Shag Rock. He threw himself across the wheel, straining with all his strength, but the pull was irresistible. They were heading smack into the rock.

Leyne, at first unaware of the danger of the situation, was suddenly alerted and screamed as the boat lurched. The deck then sloped so acutely that she was tossed onto her side and rolled over as she clutched the legs of a bench seat to prevent herself being flung overboard.

They were going straight for the rock. Gray gripped the steering like a vice, feeling there was nothing more he could do. He suddenly saw the symbols on the tusk as clearly as if with his physical eyes and sensed their presence. He knew he had only to draw them in the air. But dare he loose the steering? They were going to crash anyway. It would only take a second.

As he let go of the steering and began to draw the symbols the boat started to twist madly. The sea tossed and turned it as if it was a child's spinning top. Then miraculously the throbbing in his head ceased, the boat righted itself and with only seconds to spare they were clear. They were safe, and as they passed Gugh's massive outcrop the lights of St Mary's could be seen in the distance.

Once into harbour, he pushed and pulled his aunt up the steep stone steps in the rain that was now pelting down, wondering for the umpteenth time why they still hadn't bothered to come into the twenty-first century to provide suitable access for the disabled. Then she waited on the quay-side under cover of the eaves of the waiting room, firmly closed at this time of night, while he went off to alert the landlord of the Mermaid who came down to the quay in a buggy to collect her. Gray reflected that it was lucky it was the end of October or there wouldn't have been accommodation for her just at the drop of a hat.

As he sailed back across the Sound he felt his fear return. Every sound, every wave lashing up from the sea seemed to hold a threat. If only time could go backwards. If only he could turn the clock back to when none of this had happened. Perhaps Dad could have learned to join in more with the rest of the community. Perhaps everything could have been different, they wouldn't have been so disliked. But that wasn't possible.

He knew he'd changed. It wasn't that he was blaming Dad, the way he'd lived so separate, so self-contained. It was just that he didn't feel that way of life was right for him anymore. He still wanted his freedom to come and go as he pleased, but underneath it all was a longing to be accepted, a deep longing to prove that he was worthy of riding out to sea in the eight man gig, straining at the oars with the best of them. He knew he was strong and fit enough. It was a feeling of wanting to be a participant and at the same time free of others' opinions. Perhaps it was true that things could change in a day, in the twinkling of an eye. He wondered if the change in him had anything to do with his meeting Julie.

$$*\qquad*\qquad*\qquad*$$

The wind had stilled and the storm, like the frequently changing moods of island weather, had passed over by the time Gray pulled into Periglis Bay. There had been no hint of the pulsating sensations in his body as he passed Shag Rock at the outermost edge of the island. But he couldn't dismiss the fact that someone on the island was now in possession of the tusk. Despite what he'd said to Julie he was convinced that his father's disappearance, the strange behaviour of the sea creatures, the birds and the reported effects on shipping around St Hellicks, were connected with it and he feared how it might now be used in the wrong hands. Hadn't he experienced himself the extraordinary power of the tusk's symbols? He had felt empowered by them. They had appeared to work for, not against, him. But who knew how the tusk would respond to those with greedy minds?

The house seemed eerily still, quiet and cold. Gray decided it wasn't only the draught blowing through the wooden slats nailed over the kitchen window. It was more a feeling of desertion that had settled on the house. He felt empty inside. He remembered how he'd felt as he'd sailed back home. Yes, he was free, wasn't he? Just as Dad had always wanted to be. Free of everyone. And suddenly it didn't feel good to be that free.

Dad was no longer there to guide him, nor Rob with his brotherly jibes. There was no Tom, nor Charlotte, not even Aunt Aleyne. And no Julie, either. She'd go away at the end of the week, back to the mainland, never giving him another thought.

Gray had an overwhelming desire to talk to someone, anyone, in a way he'd never felt before. In the past all his confessions, his hopes, his frustrations had been shared with the rocks and boulders on Burnt Island. Right now that wasn't what he wanted. Anyway, the tide was in and the connecting causeway was covered by the sea.

I could phone Julie. But why? What would I say? It's only a few hours since I left. I couldn't tell her about the fire and the tusk. It would make me sound such a wimp.

He looked in the cupboard for something to eat. He felt ravenously hungry. There were several tins of soup and a tin of beans, which he opened and ate cold. He turned on the radio and then switched it off again. He couldn't settle.

Perhaps if he walked down to St Warna's he might call the seals. But they wouldn't respond at this time of night—they would be sure to be away basking somewhere. Yet it was worth a try.

The moon was riding high again and the sky had cleared. Although he knew the track so well he could have gone there blindfolded he was glad of the light. And the light from Bishop sweeping across his path was somehow comforting.

When he came over the ridge and looked down on the bay the sea was rolling in gently. He whistled in a way the seals always answered to and waited. He waited a long time but they didn't appear. He thought of whistling them up again but it seemed unfair to call them from their basking.

Gray had just decided to go back home when he spotted first one round black head and then another and another pushing through the water, sleek and shiny in the moonlight. He ran down to the edge of the sea as they swished towards him like dogs answering their master. With quivering muzzles and their huge round eyes watching him they sidled up the beach towards him.

He could talk to them, knowing they couldn't answer but felt they understood him in some deep, mysterious way. "What did happen to Dad and Rob out there the night of the storm?" he asked them. The largest bull seal grunted as if trying to communicate while the two others looked on with wide watchful eyes. "They didn't drown, did they? Did they manage to get to shore, to the mainland?"

There was silence except for the sound of the sea shivering over the shingle … *shshs* … *cash* … *sserre* … *us* … *ass* … *eruss.*

Casserus, or Casseritides. The sea was whispering to him. Was he imagining the sound of the name? Reliving his aunt's fears as well as his own?

But why, if Dad did get back to shore, would he have left him alone not knowing what had happened? That couldn't be true. It hurt too much to bear thinking about.

"Perhaps I should go away too. What's left here for me?"

Again the bull seal grunted and shuffled his heavy glistening body over to a hard flat rock as the others dived back into the sea.

Gray watched them, seeing their joy of plunging back into their natural element. On land they were ungainly, movement was difficult, but back in the water they became curving, graceful acrobats twisting, turning and slicing though the waves with great ease. And then he understood what they were telling him.

You're more alive watching us dance in the sea, watching the sea sucking in through the rocks and gullies than anywhere else in the world. And you're here on this island, in your own element for a reason … for a reason …

And again he heard the swishing sound of the incoming tide like the sound of a name, *Casserus, Casseritides.*

He was so lost in thought he didn't hear a voice calling him. It was not until he felt someone touch his shoulder that he started and looked up to see Jed Rowe speaking to him.

Jed sounded annoyed. "There's been some burning going on. Was it you? You know the rules. Have you been burning some rubbish, lad?"

Gray shook his head, not trusting himself to speak about the night's events, not even knowing whether he would be believed.

"I came over a while ago when I smelt burning and I thought I saw some black smoke coming from a bonfire, but when I looked for you and your boat, I mean Tom's, it was gone."

"I was away to St Mary's taking my aunt back there."

"Were you now?"

Even in the half light Gray could see Jed's furrowed brow and the doubt in his eyes.

"A right barney she's caused reporting folks to the Customs. Doesn't she know we don't like sneaks here? She's not welcome any more."

"She won't be back. She's gone. Leaves for the mainland in the morning."

"Ah! So she sets up trouble and then shoots off, eh? I never did believe that tale about someone drowning her cat. Who'd do that anyway? She took the law into her own hands and we don't do things that way."

Jed was a sort of headman on the island. Besides being the only vet he was called upon to be part time doctor, postman, and upholder of the law, but even so his tone riled Gray into saying. "But some, like the Trevericks, do."

"Watch what you're saying, young man," said Jed, gripping his shoulder firmly.

Gray stood up, shaking Jed's hand off.

"I know what I'm saying. They set fire to our kitchen."

"No!" Jed looked dumbfounded. "They wouldn't do that."

"Well, they did, and my aunt was scared, and that's why she's gone," Gray said in one breath.

Jed said, "Humph".

And Gray knew he wasn't believed.

"You'd have done well to have gone with her yourself if you're going to go on making these accusations. What your aunt did telling the Customs was bad, not just bad, wicked. Perhaps worse even than what you've done."

"Me?" Gray, puzzled, screwed up his forehead.

"Don't pretend you don't know why folks are saying the herd at Higher Farm are ailing, why the catch is poor and why the migrants are giving us a miss."

"You really think that's because of me? That's Agnes Treverick's tale-telling. Surely *you* don't believe her and her idea about curses? My Dad was only joking the day he said he hoped her boys would be bitten in their sleep."

"Most times I'm a reasonable man, lad, you know that, but I've been watching you. I never knew anyone who could call up the seals like you did just then and at this time of night when they never ever show. It's not natural. It was like you were talking to them and they understood you. In my book that's weird. It's more than weird. It's the kind of spookiness folks don't like on St Hellick's."

Gray was amazed that his empathy with the seals could be interpreted in this way, yet he didn't feel that Jed was really against him. But he wasn't for him, either. He was kind of neutral. He supposed that was how he should be because he was headman, so unlike Tom who'd always understood him and had taken his side.

"You wouldn't know how we folk feel." Jed shifted his gaze and looked out to sea. "There's a lot of superstition about the creatures of the sea and about the sea itself. It's our nurturer but it's also our enemy. It takes away from us as much as it gives and we don't meddle with it. You don't belong, like we belong. The Rowes have been here hundreds of years and the Hendersons, the Jenkins and the Trevericks. Maybe everyone here's family of a sort. In many cases real blood family. We're like shoals of fish in the sea or flocks of birds in the air, all of one mind. You can't change that. You mainlanders will never understand that."

Gray knew it was hopeless but he couldn't accept what he was being accused of and he was determined to make Jed believe he'd been sorely treated.

"So it was right to burn my house and steal my belongings?" Gray persisted.

"Oh? What was stolen then?"

Gray had the feeling that Jed knew already.

"Something I found by the shore."

"That wouldn't be stealing now, would it, lad? Everything from the sea is ours by rights. You'll find we stick together. No-one ever betrays anyone else to outsiders. I'm surprised after all the time you've lived here you've never noticed." Jed turned to follow the inland track and as they parted ways Gray felt a net was closing around him.

And all the while he could hear the sea whispering louder and louder, unmistakeably whispering over and over that nightmarish word *Casseritides*.

✳   ✳   ✳   ✳

"How's yer aunt?"

Gray nearly jumped out of his skin.

Agnes Treverick was blocking his way ahead on the coastal track. He couldn't sidestep her as the banks on either side were heavy with prickly gorse and tall ferns. What the devil was she doing here? People rarely ventured to this side of the island after dark. What could the old witch be up to? In the half-light she looked uglier than usual with her squat stocky figure, gaping mouth and broken teeth.

Gray remained silent but all the time was thinking how he might get her to admit to having stolen the tusk.

"It's nigh on two months since yer dad and brother went away," she went on in a sinister tone.

"They didn't go away. They were drowned." Gray knew the gossip she was spreading around the island saying that they'd deliberately disappeared.

"Nay lad, drowned folk'd be washed up somewhere by now," she said pursing her lips together tightly which emphasised the lines running between her nose and upper lip, and which in the moonlight, looked for all the world like black spiders' legs.

"Perhaps you'd please mind your own business," said Gray, glaring at her with profound dislike.

"Oh! And I take it that your aunt is minding her own business?"

"As a matter of fact she is. You …," he hesitated, his normal lack of vulgarity preventing the swear word that hovered on his lips.

"Well then, two of us can play the Customs' game," she said edging nearer, her small, close-together eyes shooting venom at him.

He shivered. He understood her exactly.

"I remember someone asking me to price an object out of pure curiosity," she said tartly. "An object he'd never set eyes on."

She watched him with a growing intensity as if waiting for his fear to show.

But Gray kept his cool, reasoning that if the tusk were now in their possession, the Trevericks wouldn't be able to prove he was the one who'd failed to report it. She was baiting him, like a small terrier, just vainly yapping away.

"But isn't arson a much more serious offence?" he said, hoping the thrust would strike home.

Her eyes narrowed as he pushed past her on the track.

"You can't stick that one on us. Don't you try it. You with your so-called magic tricks. The others might be afraid of you but not me. I've more magic tricks in my little finger than in yer whole body. Ye want to be careful too, walking out here o' dark nights. Them crevices atween the rocks is mighty dangerous. Ye could fall in an' never be found again. I've heard tell as …"

But Gray cut her short with "Are you threatening me?"

She gave a nasty cackling sound.

Gray didn't wait to hear any more. He was already bounding over the stile at the end of the track and was hurrying home as fast as he could.

CHAPTER 18

▼

Gray was shivering by the time he reached the farmhouse. Inured as he was to wading in icy cold seas he knew the cold and trembling in his limbs was due to sheer exhaustion. Within the space of twenty-four hours he'd lost lifelong friends, his last remaining relative, handled a boat alone for the first time, been the object of theft and arson, and he was now under suspicion by Jed, the only islander who might have shown him understanding.

He flung open the farmhouse door. The telephone in the hall met his eye. He wanted desperately to ring Julie. The thing, covered in a shroud of soot, stared at him obstinately tempting him. Before he realised what he was doing he'd lifted the receiver. It was almost midnight. What was he thinking of? James would be justified in believing him wild, uncivilised. However, the repeated bleep indicated someone had left a message.

A bland voice purred, "You were called today at 6.45."

He dialled callback and heard Julie's lilting voice. "Coming over in the morning. Granp's is away on a conference."

He replaced the receiver and stopped shivering for the first time. He picked up the receiver again just to have the luxury of hearing Julie's voice once more.

Gray remembered the white sandals. This time he would dare to give them to her. He hoped they were still safely in *Sea Rover's* cabin where he'd left them. It was too late now, but he would go to rescue them first thing in the morning.

He helped himself to a can of coke from a collection of tins in a cupboard that had escaped the worst of the fire. He was just considering what an almighty explosion there would have been if the cupboard had caught alight when something, a sound from the landing above, stopped him mid-thought. He carefully put the can down on the kitchen table and moved silently towards the foot of the stairs.

From above came a pattering sound, moving to and fro and then it ceased. Mice, he thought. Then came a louder sound as though something had been knocked over and the pattering continued, but it now appeared to be moving across the ceiling, or floor of the adjoining bedroom.

His heart beating furiously, he began to climb the stairs, when suddenly a black furry shape flew at him. He staggered under the unexpected missile, keenly aware of the fusty, musty stench of cat as the creature clung on to him with its claws.

"Co'burn!" he cried out in terror. It was certainly no spectral vision—it was far too solid and audible. It screeched and scrabbled away at him with its paws. He shook himself free with a sort of distaste but the animal having landed safely on the next step began to purr softly. It climbed up beside him and began to rub against his leg.

If this was indeed Co'burn then what had he buried behind the barn?

*   *   *   *

That night Gray, fearing fresh reprisals, lay fully clothed on the settee in the lounge still reeking of smoke. His strange companion lay curled up by his feet. Sooty cobwebs dangled eerily from the blackened ceiling and Gray felt that something else had crept into the house with the smoke and the spectral cat. Something that had wiped out his once carefree life, something sinister and unspeakable which was casting a shadow over the whole island.

He slept fitfully and dreamt he was with Julie on Gugh Island. She was mocking him about his ability to speak to the seals and the ancient stones. He was trying to tell her that it wasn't anything special or to be feared but she brushed past him crying out that he was possessed of an evil spirit. At that moment the vast leaning stone known as the Old Man of Gugh began to move and Julie screamed in terror as the stone appeared to take on the shape of an old monk in hooded robes. In sepulchral tones the monk uttered the words:

"The waters will not come again ... again ... again ..."

Gray woke, the words echoing in his head, his forehead covered in sweat. Somewhere in the distance he could hear a deep repeated moaning sound. He sprang up as the cat leapt from beside him, unbolted the door and saw a thick white milky mist shrouding the yard. The sound, like the sound of a cow in labour, came again and he realised it was the foghorn warning shipping to keep clear of the dangerous rocks and reefs surrounding St Hellicks.

There was no hope of Julie coming over now.

The cat meowed piteously.

"What am I to do with you? There can't be much milk left in the fridge." Gray was surprised to see how glossy the cat's fur looked and how well fed he appeared. "Someone must have been feeding you all this while. You've been too spoilt to fend for yourself."

Co'burn meowed even louder. This was no ghost.

When the Trevericks threw the drowned cat at me I'm sure they wanted me to believe it was Co'burn. They must have believed it too. Co'burn was the only cat on the island, I'm certain of that. Another thing that's odd—Co'burn was driven mad by the tusk and now it's gone missing he's come back. What can it all mean?

Gray shook his head in bafflement. He opened the fridge and found that there was still half a bottle of milk and a packet of cat's biscuits. He poured the milk into a saucer and scooped the biscuits into another dish. He was about to fry himself a couple of eggs when he heard the phone.

It was Julie.

"What's the weather like over there?" she said.

"Mist's so thick I can't see as far as the barn."

"It's lifting here and they say it'll be clear by lunch time, so I guess I'll be coming over. That's if you still want to see me."

Gray's pulse quickened. Did he ever?

"I've tons to tell you and ..." he hesitated, "I've got a present for you."

Doh, that's torn it. I'll have to give her the sandals now and she's going to hate them.

He decided to mix the eggs with the rest of the milk and make an omelette.

"Well, my friend," he said to the cat who was licking his paws, "we'll have to go down to Jed's and get some fresh milk for Julie."

How things change! He'd almost hated the animal and now he was chatting away to it, so friendly. The change, he thought, had happened about the same time that his aunt had started to behave more like a human being.

He wondered if *he* would ever change his attitude towards the Trevericks. And he shuddered when he recalled the cruel comments Agnes had made about his dad. Never a day passed without him thinking about Dad and Rob. The pain was still there, but it was now more of a dull ache. He'd never really given up hope of seeing them again.

The omelette had browned, or blackened, more than he expected and he scraped it out onto a plate. Fortunately he was very hungry and couldn't afford to be choosy about his lack of cooking expertise.

After soaking the burnt pan in the sink he looked around at the sooty walls and wondered how he could possibly invite Julie here. Perhaps they could lunch at the pub. Aunt Aleyne had left him some money and had promised to send more once she was settled back on the mainland. All of which reminded him that his aunt would not have left St Mary's yet.

He resisted his first generous thought of phoning The Mermaid to tell his aunt about Co'burn. She would be sure to come rushing back and that was the last thing he wanted. Co'burn could always be sent ahead via steerage once she was settled.

Time to get the sandals, he thought as he pulled on his anorak, failing to notice Co'burn sneak past him as he opened the door.

The hedgerows were thick with dew and draped in white hoary cobwebs on all the tracks leading down to the old quay. Pearly drops of mist hung on the gate by the churchyard. It was still difficult to see across the bay.

As Gray stepped onto the quay and prepared to climb down into the dinghy two shadowy yet familiar shapes emerged from behind the church wall, stopped, hesitated and then flung up their arms and yelled a loud "Arh ... r ... r ... gh!" Then, taking off, they were soon swallowed up by the mist.

Bemused, Gray frowned, until he heard a deep purr which he interpreted later as one of pure satisfaction. There, with the white mist shrouding his fur, was Co'burn, as ghostly a creature as anyone could wish.

"Good work Co'burn! I bet the Trevericks were stoned out of their minds."

He threw a piece of bread from his pocket to the cat who slid down onto his haunches, nibbling and watching Gray as he rowed through the now lifting mist towards *Sea Rover*.

CHAPTER 19

▼

By lunchtime the mist had lifted and the pale rays of a watery sun were penetrating the clouds.

Gray decided to take the tractor down to Porth Conger to meet the midday boat.

He thought of leaving Co'burn locked up inside the house for his own safety. But the creature scrabbled and scratched at the door and meowed so loudly he changed his mind and let him out into the yard, whereupon the cat dived under the hedge next to the barn and disappeared from sight.

Gray began to search for him and was reminded by the clucking of the hens and grunting of the pigs that he had forgotten their feed. He cursed himself for his carelessness but there was no time now, he couldn't be late meeting Julie. He stowed the carefully wrapped sandals in the inside pocket of his anorak and climbed up into the tractor's cabin.

The boat was on time and Gray watched as the handful of passengers disembarked. But he couldn't see Julie anywhere. Then he made out a slim figure with dark hair engaged in conversation with one of the boatmen. His heart leapt as he recognised Julie's familiar way of flicking back her hair with her hand.

She picked up her haversack from the storage area and, flinging it over her shoulder, bounded up the steep slope towards the tractor.

"Isn't this fab," she said as she clambered up into the cabin beside Gray. "A whole day to ourselves without Granps fussing. I adore him but he's constantly telling me to take care. Oops! Forgot about that aunt of yours."

"No worries," grinned Gray. "Aunt Aleyne won't be around."

"Oh?"

"I'll tell you later. Now, would you like to eat here at the pub?"

"No. I've a much better idea. Everything we need is in here." She patted her haversack. "Why don't we go over to that bay of yours, you know, the one with the seals and have lunch there?"

"A great idea. But first I'll have to see to the animals and check up on Co'burn. Do you mind?"

"Can I help? I'd love to ... but you said Co'burn. Wasn't that what your aunt's cat was called, the one that was drowned?"

Gray said "hmm," and wondered how he was going to explain.

"He reappeared suddenly last night scaring me solid," he said. "I'm still not sure whether he's some kind of phantom, but he seems real enough. His 'drowning' was one of the reasons my aunt has gone, or is going back to the mainland, today. She's over on St Mary's waiting for the afternoon boat."

"Weird," said Julie, sinking into a thoughtful reverie.

"Even weirder, the Treverick boys, you remember the ones who chased us the day we went over to Gugh, brought the drowned cat up to the farm."

"That couldn't have been your aunt's cat. How could it? It could have been any old cat."

"Hardly. If you remember, this is a bird sanctuary."

"Well, it could have been a ship's cat got drowned and was washed up."

"Hmm!"

"You're not making this up are you?"

They had reached the farm by now and as they drove into the yard Julie, seeing the blackened window and door of the farmhouse, exclaimed, "Grief! Have you had a fire?"

"Yes, and I didn't make that up either."

Julie opened the cabin door, jumped out and began examining the door and the window. "How did it start?"

"It didn't just *start*. Someone started it. I've got my suspicions ... more than suspicions. My aunt actually saw the Trevericks, but by then it was too late to stop them."

"Revenge? A bit extreme, don't you think?" Julie shook her head and frowned. "There's a lot about this island that doesn't make sense. Look, I told you that Granps went off last night to the mainland to a conference?"

Gray nodded.

"He said that the SIPP, who are holding the conference, are intrigued by certain phenomena surrounding this island and are wondering how to set up experiments to discover the causes."

"I remember him talking about it. Is that why you're here? Spying out the land?" he joked. "Now I know why you want to go to seal bay to see how really unhinged I am?"

"Come on! You're not serious. I think you're different, interesting, maybe a bit mysterious, but never crazy. But it doesn't mean I'm not aware of the strangeness of this place. It sort of grabs you as soon as you set foot here. I mean, look at all those weird rocks shaped like animals all over the place. It's spooky, makes me shiver, but it's thrilling."

"To me, it's a magical place."

"Not according to Granps. There's something very wrong here."

"How? What exactly does he mean?"

"Let's feed your animals and I'll tell you more as we walk down to the bay. Come on!"

Julie skipped from time to time as they walked across the Downs, finding it impossible to match her steps to Gray's huge stride.

"Slow down!" she said with a breathy laugh.

"Sorry! I'm so used to haring across here on my own."

"I'll never find enough breath to talk if you don't."

"Sit here for a while then." He pulled off his anorak and spread it on the flattened top of a stone outcrop overlooking the sea. "Now, tell me what your Grandfather thinks is going on."

"You know that the organisation he belongs to is about recording unusual psychic events?"

Gray nodded.

"That's really why he came over before to find out if your aunt had unearthed anything new about the lost land of Casseritides."

"Um, yes?"

"Well, the SIPP were still not sure whether the strange magnetic power of the sunken land was the cause of the high level of radiation around St Hellicks, or whether it was something new, something more sinister. They had already dowsed the ley lines, the earth's magnetic energy lines, and found something was reactivating them. One of the members had a one-year-old Irish wolfhound which suddenly began to thrash around wildly and have seizures when his owner was measuring levels of radiation travelling across the Sound from the direction of St Hellicks." She paused and lowered her tone mysteriously, "And they found that something was actually affecting the animal's brain-waves."

Gray looked startled. "Maybe that's what happened to Co'burn. He went crazy and bit Aunt Aleyne; then he shot off for days."

"So," Julie continued, "because there has been a growing increase in the levels detected, they've invited a group of scientists to the conference. Granps and his friends have got this strong feeling that it's more than the usual magnetic effect commonly experienced round these islands and might be due to some kind of technology or radiation spill ... and I thought," she hesitated.

"Oh! What did you think?"

Julie looked at him without blinking. "Can't you guess?"

Gray snorted. "The tusk? You don't give up, do you? You can't really believe it has anything to do with this radiation idea. Anyway, it's all so vague. A dog has fits and a cat goes crazy. They're probably not in the least bit connected."

"And that's what you want to believe?"

"I mean, I don't know for sure. It wasn't until I met you and your Grandfather that I started thinking maybe the tusk did have more far reaching effects. And later I actually experienced it reaching out to me with its power."

"And then?"

"And then I stopped it."

Julie looked at him, eyes wide with interest.

"You stopped its power? How? Oh never mind now. What matters, is, could you still stop it?"

"Maybe. But I might be too late. Perhaps I could only stop its power affecting me. I somehow feel connected to it. I mean, I was the one who found it. It was like a message, a personal message just for me. Or maybe it was a message for the whole island. I don't know. Perhaps with someone else who it's not meant for, it acts differently. Now it's nothing to do with me anymore anyway. It's been stolen."

"Stolen?" Julie frowned.

"I found out last night. In fact, shortly after the Trevericks tried to burn down the farm."

"And you think they stole it?"

"I'm not a hundred percent certain. But I know it's still on the island because I've felt its vibrations. Also, I met Agnes Treverick who as much as said they had it. It's probably stashed away in their shop by now."

"Then," she rounded on him sharply, "you've got to get it back. Granps says the increased levels of radiation could have far reaching effects. If the tusk is the cause, you've got to do something about it."

"How? Even if they do have it, what do you think I can do? Politely go and ask for it back? Some hopes!"

"We don't need to get it back right now. Just find out if they've got it. But some things are more immediately urgent, like lunch. I'm ravenous." And Julie began to open the haversack and take out chickens' legs carefully wrapped in grease proof paper, tomatoes, bags of crisps, apples and a bottle of lemonade.

Just as they were finishing their meal Julie exclaimed, "Isn't that your cat?"

Sure enough, Co'burn came scampering over the mossy ground with a half eaten bird or fish between his jaws.

"Drop it, you little devil," said Gray getting to his feet and giving chase. "As if we haven't enough trouble without that." But Co'burn shot off at great speed and Gray returned to Julie with a scowl on his face.

"So that's how he kept alive while he was missing."

"He just went back to his natural wild state." Julie tapped her lips. "That's given me an idea."

"What?"

"Cat Burglary." She smiled at his look of utter disbelief. "Cat burglars are sly and cunning, they slip into places undetected and slip out again. They always leave everything exactly as it was. So no-one ever knows they've been there. If anything's missing the owners simply think they must have misplaced it."

"You're crazy! How are you going to get into the shop, if that's where it is, and out again, carrying a metre long tusk?"

"I'm not. I'm just going to slip in quietly and have a look around. If I'm spotted I can always say I'm looking to buy a present and this Agnes woman doesn't know me. But Granps has taught me one or two tricks about appearing 'invisible'. I'll be as soft footed and stealthy as Co'burn."

"And then?"

"If they have got it, we let the SIPP know and take it from there."

"Talking about being soft footed, I told you I had a present for you." Gray ferreted in his anorak's inside pocket and drew out the carefully wrapped package. He blushed slightly as he offered it her.

"Wow! They're an exact fit," she said as she slipped her bare feet into the snowy white leather shoes. "How on earth did you guess?"

"That's my secret."

"Now I shall be a soft white Persian cat burglar. Thanks, they're *puurrfect.*" They both laughed. "When do I start?"

"The shop's usually busy only directly after a boat comes in with new visitors or just before it leaves. People go there to browse around while waiting for the boat. Things could be quiet right now but we'll have to risk it."

"Okay, let's go."

CHAPTER 20

▼

"I'm going to hide here in the ditch under the tamarisk hedge," said Gray. "Any hint of trouble and I'll be out like a shot. Remember, Agnes is deaf, so she won't hear the door chimes as you open the door but she's installed an ingenious device. As you enter, a huge stuffed cormorant bats you in the face. Most people scream so she knows someone has come into the shop."

"Do you really feel the tusk is in there?" asked Julie tremulously.

"Yes, I can feel the vibrations now. Are you sure you can't feel it too?"

"Nope. Not a thing, except the butterflies in my stomach."

"You don't have to do this. These people are not playing games and it could turn nasty. Look, we'll think of another way to find out."

"No way. Once I make up my mind nothing can stop me. And if we don't try now the tusk might just get spirited off some place else. What exactly am I looking for?"

"You won't have any difficulty recognising it because of its length. It is ivory coloured and around its whole length the shape twists like a serpent. On its side are carved many old runic symbols. When I copied these for the first time I felt incredibly powerful and strong."

"I wish I did right now," said Julie. "I can't stop trembling."

Gray put his arm round her and said, "I'll draw the symbols over you. It may work for you too."

As precisely as he could remember them Gray drew the symbols in the air above Julie, the one shaped like a star, then the half diamond, the ring of spindles, the rake and the hooks, the triangles and the double pyramids while Julie looked on apprehensively.

"Did you sense anything?" he asked.

She shrugged. "Not sure."

"Can you tell me how you're feeling now?"

"Sort of calm, not as jittery."

"Good! I think the symbols have some kind of protective power. That's how they feel to me. Remember this is no ordinary shop and the tusk is not likely to be on display. You will have to ferret around and there's more junk there than you could possibly imagine in your wildest dreams. But if it's there, and I'm sure it is, you'll find it."

"I hope you're right. Okay. See you soon." And she walked bravely towards the shop, opened the door and disappeared from view.

*   *   *   *

It was chilly lying in the ditch and drops of moisture dripped constantly from the hedge down Gray's neck and he was seized with violent cramps but he remained at his post with his ears pricked alert and ready for any sign of Julie' s voice. He found himself praying. The words were strangely religious and old fashioned. He didn't know at first where the words had come from as his father had not brought him up in any form of religion. They seemed to come from a far distant time and as he lay there he had a sudden recollection of the gentleness of a mother he thought he'd long forgotten. In an odd sort of way it seemed to him like some kind of warning, as though the ghost of his long lost mother was trying to protect him from or hint at some danger he was in. He shivered and then the idea faded and he saw Julie crouching down and telling him to get up.

"It was there," she said in an excited voice, "but I think I've been seen. Come on, there's no time to waste."

They raced back to the farmhouse. As Gray turned his key in the lock he heard a distant shout and guessed they had been pursued and once they were both inside he drew the bolts.

"Quickly, upstairs to the attic," he said, leading the way. "The windows look out over the coast track and the farmyard. We'll soon spot if anyone's been following."

Sure enough, the heads of both Treverick boys came into view. Julie was shivering and so Gray drew her closer. The words of the prayer came into his head once again and at that moment the most amazing thing happened. Co'burn padded into the yard, saw his two enemies, the boys who'd thrown his basket into the hedge on his arrival on the island, and spitting venomously flew at them as viciously and as ferociously as Gray ever remembered. And once again, as if pursued by the spectre of the drowned cat, the boys yelled and took to their heels.

"That was one amazing spectre," laughed Julie. "I can just imagine the Trevericks if they believed it was Co'burn's ghost. What a great idea to come up here to get a bird's eye view."

She looked around at the books spread higgedly piggedly all over the shelves and the floor.

"Sorry about the mess," said Gray. "Aunt Aleyne threw them out and I haven't had chance to sort them."

"Yours?" she queried. "I thought you said you didn't go to school."

"They're Dad's. But that doesn't mean I can't read. Dad was an excellent teacher, but I'm much better at drawing and making things. Look, you're still shivering. There isn't much in the house but I can make you a hot drink, then you can tell me exactly what happened."

Over two steaming mugs of hot chocolate they shared the events of the afternoon.

"I really shouldn't have let you do it," said Gray. "There was always the danger that Rod Treverick would see and recognise you and putting two and two together guess why you were there."

"I'm glad you warned me about the cormorant, otherwise I think I would have screamed. There was no one in the shop so I looked around but could see nothing huge enough to be the tusk. From the window I could see the steps up to the cottage next to the shop and the door was open. I went up the steps and looked inside. A short stocky woman in an apron was cooking something on the stove in the kitchen. She had her back to me. And then I saw it. In a corner of the room wrapped in a blanket there was something that looked suspiciously tall. I crept in as quiet as a mouse and pulled apart the folds of the blanket. My guess was right—it was the tusk. I didn't stop to re-arrange the blanket but crept out just as quietly, certain that I hadn't been noticed. But as I left the cottage I saw the Treverick boys coming up from the quay and I knew they'd seen me."

"But there's no reason why they should think you were looking for the tusk."

"Then why did they follow me?"

"Because you're a very pretty girl."

Julie blushed and punched him playfully. "Well, now we know where the tusk is, what now?"

"I'm not as convinced as you that it is so important."

"Well, I think it is. And I'm sure the SIPP will think so too."

"I'm not going down that way. It scares me to think of it. What if it's true that it did have something to do with disturbing fishing and causing boats to become disoriented or lost? What if ..." he paused and his face looked drawn and pale, "what if it did have something to do with Dad's disappearance?"

Julie placed a hand on his arm. "That's good, isn't it? I mean, it could be something to hang on to, something to hope for, like discovering a clue."

Gray sighed. "How can it be a clue? There's a whole ocean out there to be searched, stretching from here to America. How can anything help? They're lost and nothing's ever going to bring them back. Do you think I haven't asked every day and begged God, if there is such a thing, to find them?"

"Someone once told me that every prayer and everything you really ask for is heard and answered in some way or other."

"Rubbish Julie! I don't want an answer in 'some way or other' as you put it. I want my Dad and brother back here, not some sort of consolation prize dished out by the universe. Alright, I admit I've begged damn hard but what good is that?"

"Honest, I don't know. But," she said emphatically, "I do know this tusk is going to tell us something. Perhaps that's the 'other way'. Perhaps we've not got to be blinkered by thinking answers only come in the way we expect but we should look for them all the time, believing they're there, trusting they're there and just being persistent enough to find them. Never, never giving up."

"I haven't given up, believe me, but I'm still scared."

"I wish Mum was here. She'd know what to do. She's always talking about wanting to come to the islands but she never does."

"But why? Your grandfather has a house on **St** Mary's. Why doesn't she come over?"

"They quarrelled years ago over my Stepfather. Granps could never forgive Mum for marrying him after my real father, Granp's son, died. They've never spoken to each other since."

"But *you* visit."

"Yep, I'm like a sort of go-between, taking messages from one to the other. They'd never communicate otherwise."

"She could come to stay here?" Gray reddened. "I mean, you could both stay here."

"At the farm?"

"There's a self catering flat. Look, I'll get the key and you can see for yourself," said Gray, opening the drawer where the key was kept. "That's odd. It's not here. Aunt Aleyne was the last to use it. I wonder where she put it?"

"Never mind, we can look through the window. It wouldn't matter if it was just a shed I'd persuade her to come, then we could go sailing together, you and me. And oh! What great fun!" Her eyes were shining with excitement. "But," she glanced at her wristwatch. "Jeez! Look at the time. I've got to go. I don't know when Granps' flight is due but he'll hit the roof if I'm not there when he gets back."

"Even more so if he knows where you've been I guess. I get the feeling he doesn't really approve of me."

"I'm not exactly going to tell him. I'll just casually mention I've spoken to you on the phone and drop in a hint about the tusk."

"You'd better change out of the sandals then or he'll start asking awkward questions. And, you've already missed the last boat back."

"Oh damn!"

"I'll take you in *Sea Rover*. I was going to anyway."

"That's great!" She gave him a huge grin. "You're right about the sandals," she said, slipping them off and placing them carefully inside her haversack. "Granps doesn't miss a trick. You still haven't told me how you knew my size."

"I measured the footprints you left in the muddy field."

"You what?"

"Then I made a pattern, cut them out of leather and sewed them."

"Whew! I don't get it? You sewed them yourself?"

"Yes. That's what Dad did. He made shoes. That's how he made a living. He taught us, me and Rob."

"Wow! And you made them yourself. For *me?*"

Gray looked down.

"Do you know that's the nicest thing anybody's ever done for me. I mean ever!" She stood on tiptoes and kissed him.

Gray was dumbstruck, amazed, that she meant it. But all the same, he kissed her back

"Sorry," he sighed. "We do have to go in case the mist drops again."

Julie picked up her haversack and they walked side by side through the narrow lane to the old quay where he helped her into the dinghy.

"Oh look!" she laughed. Co'burn had jumped down beside her. "The demon cat's come too. I thought cats hated water."

"There's no knowing what this one likes. He's a law unto himself," said Gray as he rowed over to the boat riding at anchor in the middle of the bay.

As they came into St Mary's harbour and pulled over to the landing steps *Sea Rover* was dwarfed by a huge ship, the *Scillonian*, which gave a loud warning hoot, that it was preparing to leave for the mainland. Passengers were leaning over the ship's rails waving goodbye to friends on shore when, without warning, Co'burn jumped clear of the side of the boat and shot off and up the steps.

"Now where the blazes has he gone?" muttered Gray quickly tying up the boat.

There was a loud yell of delight and Gray, looking up, recognised his aunt's vast shape racing across the deck pushing other passengers out of the way. He next saw her coming down the gangway and onto the shore as the cat sprang up into her arms.

Julie was already on the quayside having followed in the wake of Co'burn. Gray bounded after her just in time to see his aunt being hustled back on deck by one of the crew.

She turned, to shout to Gray, clutching the cat to her huge bosom. "How did you find him? I knew he'd come back. I knew it."

The *Scillonian* gave an almighty hoot drowning any further chance of conversation. His aunt waved, still clutching Co'burn with her other hand. .

"Who'd have believed that," said Julie with a laugh, which soon became a frown as she noticed a helicopter circling above the harbour and starting to descend. "Sorry Gray, I'll have to scoot. Granps mustn't know where I've been today."

Gray blushed deeply when some of the passengers on board whistled as she kissed him goodbye.

As the huge liner started to back out into the Sound Julie called, "I'll phone you! Take care sailing back home, Gray!"

CHAPTER 21

▼

It was a lonely journey back and he had to keep his eyes focused ahead as the mist was now beginning to blot out all familiar sights and sounds. From time to time he put his hand to the cheek Julie had kissed and felt a glow of intense pleasure. Her utter delight at receiving the sandals had taken him by surprise. It was such a simple gift and yet she'd actually said no-one had ever given her anything so wonderful.

His spirits soared. And then, thinking about surprises, he smiled as he remembered how Co'burn's animal instinct had directed him, swift as a laser beam, straight into his owner's arms. How amazed his aunt must have felt! He guessed she was still recovering from the shock.

One thing was certain, the Trevericks would never set eyes on Co'burn again. They'd always be convinced they'd seen a ghost cat and maybe keep off his back from now on.

The boat quivered and then lurched. Time to think about them later. He needed all his powers of concentration. The mist swirled thicker and thicker, billowing in from Bishop Rock which was no longer visible as the deadly white fog rolled over the sea, moving like a thick white carpet smothering the tiny islands and reefs and slowly taking over the land to aft. He'd never make it as far as Periglis Bay if this kept up and he would have to pull into Porth Conger.

Then, the throbbing began. It was beating in time to his heart. He felt it right through his body, pulsing in his hands. It was becoming difficult to hold the steering on course. It was controlling him. It was much stronger than anything he'd ever experienced. He remembered how he'd escaped its power before by breathing deeply and drawing the symbols in the air, but he didn't dare to let go of the steering. Throb, throb, it was becoming hard to keep focused. The sound seemed to swirl in eddies through his stomach making him want to retch. His forehead pounded. His head felt as though it was splitting open as he fought against the overwhelming desire to hold his temples.

He tried to draw the symbols in his mind but he was distracted by the intense pulsating in his body. He tried again and this time had a little more success by trying not to fight the throbbing and just allowing the symbols to move as they wished. Then suddenly they were outside his head, they were alive, dancing in front of his eyes, brilliantly silver as though lit from within. Crosses, angled letters, arrowheads shining with another worldy light. Miraculously they seemed to be directing him forward. Whenever his steering wavered they hovered directly just beyond his eye line and he knew he was safe, they were guiding him. All he had to do was to follow, going forward, ever forward, as they danced before him until, with a sigh of relief, he recognised the familiar shapes of the rocks on Burnt Island emerging through the mist and knew he was home.

The phone was ringing as he unlatched the door to the farmhouse. It had to be Julie.

He picked up the phone eagerly.

"Gary?" It was a man's voice; it sounded cultured, but it had a sharp edge.

"Yes?" Gray was suddenly afraid.

"James, Julie's grandfather. I understand she visited you today."

Gray inhaled deeply and remained silent.

"By your lack of response I suppose I can take that as a yes?"

"I can't speak for Julie," Gray said at last.

"She was expressly forbidden to leave St Mary's while I was away. While she's here I am responsible for what might happen to her. She was told St Hellicks was out of bounds. I'm afraid that means she will be going back to the mainland by the first flight tomorrow."

Gray gave a deep audible sigh.

"I'd also like to know what all this nonsense is about a tusk that emits signals."

Gray did not reply.

"I told Julie, and I can assure you, that this cannot have the slightest connection with our investigations. That is utter nonsense."

Gray's recent experience with the power of the tusk made him doubt that but still he kept quiet.

"For your own safety I would suggest that you do not attempt to sail out towards the Western Isles where we have now discovered a stronger magnetic pull than ever. A warning has been issued to all shipping in the area."

As if anyone would be sailing out there in this weather, thought Gray.

"My advice to you now is to get in some provisions to last you a few days. Acting on scientific information the Island Council of St Mary's has decided to place St Hellick's in quarantine for twenty-four hours at least, starting from tomorrow. No shipping will be allowed to land at your main quay or to leave it from tomorrow at noon. We don't want to start a panic so it really is up to you not to tell others at this stage. All islanders will be notified by morning. Julie has acted foolishly but at least, as a result, you are getting the chance to have advance warning of what is going on. Oh! And one last thing. Please don't try to ring her. You would be wasting your time. I've confiscated her mobile for the time being. Goodnight Gary. I'm sure we'll get to the bottom of this soon."

James rang off.

Well! Thanks for that. Hardly the world's most sympathetic ex-vicar, thought Gray. Where on earth does he think I'm going to get extra provisions at this time of day? He searched the cupboards to see if he'd missed anything. No, there were still only a couple of tins of soup and two cans of coke. There were always vegetables to be dug up; the potatoes had been ready for days now. There were plenty of eggs from the hens and enough fodder for the animals to last for weeks. He and they wouldn't starve.

Time for his first coke.

He sprawled on the settee, where he'd last spent the night with Co'burn, and thought of Julie, wondering how she would be feeling right now. Furiously angry, he guessed. Would they ever meet again? She'd said she'd persuade her mum to come over with her to rent the flat and even though he'd known her for such a short time he knew if she'd made up her mind she'd come in spite of her grandfather.

Everywhere was muffled by fog outside and he felt oppressively closed in. He refused to allow himself to think about what tomorrow might bring. He had to keep thinking about how things could suddenly change and how wonderful it would be to have Julie back. He had to keep thinking of her, just keep thinking of her. Would the fog lift in time for her flight? James wouldn't be able to keep her mobile when she went through to the check-in. She would ring him then. He knew she would ring him then.

Just then the phone rang.

Gray stared at it not daring to pick it up. It kept ringing. He counted four and picked it up. "Shearwater Farm," he answered.

"Gray," said that warm, strong familiar voice … a voice he'd always dreamed of hearing but never really dared even to hope to hear again. It was against all possibility. "How are you, son? I'm truly, truly sorry to shock you like this but there was no other way. Rob and I are alive, just …" David Edmond was saying. "But we've got to play this carefully. We're going to need your help."

Gray collapsed back onto the settee. The blood drained from his brain. He was eddying round and round, being sucked into the bottom of a vast whirlpool. The room blackened before his eyes. He had to take a tight grip to stop himself falling into a faint.

Dad and Rob were alive. They were alive!

So many strange things had happened recently, perhaps he was dreaming, perhaps it was the effect of the throbbing and beating in his head. He was hallucinating. He was still under the influence of the tusk. But the phone was there in his hand, the sound of Dad's voice still buzzing in his ear.

"Gray? Gray, are you alright?" His dad sounded frantic. "Speak to me. Say something."

Gray tried to lick his lips that had suddenly gone dry but his mouth was parched. He could only croak "Dad" into the mouthpiece. His mind was a blank.

"I can imagine how shocked you are Gray, but just tell me, are you on your own? No one else in the house is there? What I have to say is so dangerous, I need to be sure."

"Yea, I'm alone," Gray blurted out, his head feeling so light and empty. "But where are you?"

"I can't say now. We're being tailed. Only got a few more seconds but I'll find somewhere safe to ring you later tonight. Just make sure Tom isn't there or Charlotte. Okay? Son, I'm desperately sorry about all this." Then the line went dead.

Gray replaced the receiver, picked up the empty can of coke and found his hand was shaking violently.

He didn't know what to do. Dad had said he was ringing later so he couldn't turn in for an early night as he'd promised himself. There was an extension phone in Dad's old bedroom, the one his aunt had sequestered. He'd go up there and perhaps just lie down on the bed and wait. His head was still pounding. What did Dad mean when he said he was being tailed and where could he be?

When he opened the door to the bedroom he saw that there were boxes everywhere. Aunt Aleyne had hurriedly pulled things out of the wardrobe and drawers in her haste to leave. Clothes spilled out of drawers, and boxes had been hastily crammed with books and possessions. The title of one of the books up-ended on the floor caught his attention. *Runic Inscriptions.*

Strange, he thought, that his dad and aunt should have similar reading tastes. He couldn't see that they had anything else in common. He picked the book up and began to scan it, idly at first and then with a growing eagerness as he flipped through the pages, staring in fascination at the thousands of detailed drawings. How ironic that his aunt should have the very book that might explain the symbols on the tusk and how ironic that he'd never known until this moment that such a book existed.

The open star shapes seemed to indicate central points of power. Then there were other symbols which would break locks open, end strife, bring peace, bring courage in combat. But none were exactly like those on the tusk. He closed the book in disappointment, stretched out on the bed and slowly his head sank further into the pillow and he slept.

He was awakened by the sound of two immense thuds, one that appeared to come from the outside door and the other from the other end of the yard. He switched on the bedside lamp, for the house was now in pitch darkness, jumped out of bed and remained alert, and listening. Then from below came a low whistle which faded and then came again, this time strident and continuous, piercing the blanket of fog and rising above the muffled blaring sound of the fog-horn. And immediately there was a renewed banging on the downstairs door followed by shouts of

"Get him! Get him!"

And from the other end of the yard there were shouts of, "Now, now! Time to slay the beast."

There was a loud crash and a sound like the splintering of glass which Gray thought might be the window to the flat or the one in Dad's workshop.

From the back of the house came voices murmuring which built up to a crescendo of deep throated chanting in a tongue Gray could not recognise. The chant wailed, hummed, hissed, swayed, now rising, now falling, a steadily encroaching menace creeping into the very fabric of the house.

From the very first whistle Gray was filled with terror. He was unable to think or move. Whoever it was, was determined to terrify him and him alone for some reason. Then there were two more low whistles and suddenly the chanting stopped and he could hear voices becoming muffled and distant, swallowed up by the fog. Perhaps something had disturbed the assailants. Soon all sounds had melted away and only a deadly eerie silence remained.

Later, when the phone rang again, Gray was alert but on nerve's edge. He grabbed the phone.

"Gray." His dad's voice sounded strained. "I've been worried sick about you, desperate to let you know what was happening but unable to do so. How are you really? Is everything okay?"

How could he possibly explain? His dad had returned from the dead after an absence of almost six weeks, he'd lost the only support he'd ever had, the house was under siege, indeed the whole island was under siege if James' story was right. He'd met a wonderful girl who was flying out in the morning and whom he might never see again.

"Very shaken," was all he said. "I can't find the right words to say just how I'm feeling but I'm overjoyed you're safe. How's Rob? Is he with you? Where are you?"

"Rob's here with me. We're hundreds of miles away."

"Where?" Gray persisted.

"Too dangerous to tell you. Better you don't know right now. Don't tell anyone I phoned, not Tom, not anyone. Do you understand? I've only a short time to talk to you; we've foxed our followers but it won't be for long."

"Followers?"

"You remember the night of the great storm, the night we were lost?" David Edmond said without replying to Gray's query. "We were driven miles off course and found ourselves in a remote bay off the mainland. The worst place on earth we could have landed in. We're far away from there now, but I haven't time to spell out all the details. There's something I've got to know since I fear you and the whole island might be in danger too."

How could Dad even have an inkling of what was going on. It was uncanny.

"Do you remember our lessons on Tesla, Gray?"

Gray shook his head in puzzlement. This didn't seem the time to be going over past science lessons.

"Sort of? Something about natural forces and the effects of chain reactions through setting off vibrations?"

"That's right. The Tesla effect. Tesla experimented with harnessing natural magnetic forces and creating different kinds of apparatus but he died before they could be successfully manufactured. Now such frequencies can be placed in the tiniest of objects, indeed in objects of all shapes and sizes."

A wild and crazy thought was forming in Gray's mind but Dad's voice cut in urgently.

"Can you go up into my room, Gray? I need you to find something very important."

"I'm there now."

"So, look on the second shelf near the window for a book with the title *Ancient Sites and Earth Energies*. It's the one written by Charles Vivian. Quickly now, there's no time to be lost."

"It's not there Dad."

"How do you know? You haven't had time to look."

"Charlotte moved all your books to the attic," Gray blushed at the lie but this wasn't the moment to explain what had really happened.

"She, what?" Dad's voice became distant, then silence hung in the air. "I've just spoken to Rob. He borrowed it and he thinks it's in his room. I need to know if you've seen anything like …"

The line was bad and Gray didn't catch the rest of the sentence.

"Like … what?"

"Just fetch the book, then you'll see."

"Okay. I'll go now." Gray paused, playing for time. "Does he know where it might be?" *Of course Rob doesn't blessed well know where it might be. It could be anywhere since the aunt had shifted everything around.*

There was a suppressed chortle from the other end of the phone. "You know the state of Rob's room."

"So, it'll take some time." *Perhaps more than you realise, Dad.* "Can I call you?"

"No. Too risky. Go look for it. I'll call back."

"No. Please don't ring off Dad," said Gray. There was panic in his voice.

"Are you sure you're okay? Tom and Charlotte looking after you alright?"

"They're fine," Gray gulped.

Dad! If only you knew, if only you knew.

But all he said was, "I just can't lose you again."

"Okay. I'm hanging on. But don't worry if I have to cut you off. Believe me I won't unless I'm forced to."

And of course the book was not in Rob's room. Gray knew he was going to have to pluck up courage to go out into the yard and over to the flat. Aunt Aleyne had not only cleared Dad's room but Rob's also and most of Rob's belongings had been housed there.

He picked his way through the thickening fog pungent with the smell of samphire and seawrack towards what had now become Shearwater Flat. He found himself crunching broken glass underfoot. The upper glass partition of the door was smashed and the door had been forced open. So that had been the sound of breaking glass that he'd heard. Gray went inside cautiously and switched on the light. He saw that ornaments had been swept off shelves and lay broken on the floor. Chairs and tables had been overturned and drawers ransacked. He rummaged through a pile of magazines and books but the one Dad wanted wasn't there. Who had done this and what had they been after?

CHAPTER 22

▼

Horrified by the chaos he'd found in the flat and the ominous threat of unknown assailants, Gray stumbled back across the yard to the house, rushed inside and picked up the phone.

The line was dead. He sank down on the bed, devastated.

What was going on? Dad and Rob seemed to be caught up in a spy thriller. Nothing was making sense, not the night visitors, not the scientific investigations, nor the curfew imposed by the Islands' Council.

He began to riffle through Aunt Aleyne's box of books searching for the missing book. Perhaps she may have borrowed it just by chance. But he was out of luck. There were lots of tomes on ancient history but none by Charles Vivian. Why was this book so important and why, so late at night, did Dad want to discuss a scientist who'd been dead more than half a century ago?

So preoccupied was he with his thoughts that when the phone rang it made him jump.

"Dad?" he said eagerly.

"Is that you Gary," said a familiar female voice.

"Aunt Aleyne," he choked.

"For one crazy moment I thought you said Dad."

"No, no … I said 'glad'. I was so glad someone was ringing me."

"Well, it was a very peculiar way of answering," she said suspiciously. "I wanted to thank you for finding Co'burn and bringing him over in time to catch the boat. Sorry about the lateness of the call but I didn't want to wait until morning in case I missed you. Why didn't you let me know earlier that you'd found him? Another minute and the boat would have sailed."

"I couldn't …" Gray stuttered, feeling his whole life was becoming a web of lies.

"Never mind now. Whatever happened is no longer important. He's so content to be back with me and I'm overjoyed as you can guess. Now about my belongings. I've arranged for a courier to pick them up from you to save you the trouble of taking them over to Mary's. He should be calling in the morning. I left things in a bit of a state and hope that you will see everything is parcelled up, and labelled, addressed to me, c/o Marie Merrick, 12 Broad Street, Penzance."

"In the morning?"

"Yes Gary. Does that present a problem?"

Indeed it does, he reflected. But James had said everything would not be under curfew until after noon so perhaps he'd better keep quiet. No point in telling his aunt anything at this stage. However, there was one thing for sure, his aunt was a veritable walking library of information. "Aunt, do you happen to have a book by Charles Vivian called …?"

"*Ancient Sites and Earth Mysteries,*" she interrupted. "I live and breathe it, my boy, never separated from it. Why do you ask?"

"Julie's grandfather said something about increased magnetic radiation around St Hellick's the day he visited you. Do you know why that might be?"

It was a long shot and Gray knew it. It might have nothing at all to do with why Dad was so eager to find the book but it was worth a try.

"Interesting question. Hellicks is unusual in having so many important standing stones connected as they are to major ley lines. In the past they were more than merely important, they were often vital to the survival of the people who lived there. Such stones were always constructed at power points in the earth, points which ancient peoples saw as being connected with a vast grid of other power points spread throughout the globe."

For heavens sake get to the point. Gray found he was sweating with impatience.

"How they knew this we can never be exactly sure today. Is that why you wanted to know about Charles Vivian's book? I never realised you were interested in such things"

"Was it some sort of magical power, do you think?"

"Depends what you mean by magic. They certainly inscribed what you might call magical symbols at these places or on these stones, many of which have been erased by time and many of which we now no longer have any knowledge. The writer you spoke of, Vivian, is the world's most famous collector of such symbols."

"Were there any in his book relating to Hellicks?"

"Well, yes. There is the Tau, an ancient rune from the Eddas."

"Sorry?"

"The Eddas were old Icelandic sagas. Surely you know that, boy." Gray heard her impatient click of the tongue down the line. "There's a Tau symbol inscribed on the base of the Old Man of Gugh, now almost obliterated by time and weather I'm afraid. This was regarded as the sign of a very important source of power."

Gray had a fleeting vision of the stone on Gugh, like a huge leaning molar tooth, pitted and worn by the strong winds that blew in across the Sound, its base so encrusted with grey lichen it would be impossible to find any markings there.

"What was the meaning of it? I mean, how did people use it in the past?"

And Gray was then sorry he'd asked as she rambled on again.

"It was only entrusted to the chief of the clan and he would tap into its magic to increase his own power and to strengthen his hold over the minds of his tribe"

"Do you mean he controlled their minds, like some sort of hypnotist?"

"Who can say at what level symbols work? But certainly only he would be allowed to wear the symbol. It would be embroidered on his clothes, engraved on his weapons. He would, by taking control of it, have ultimate control over their lives."

"Weird."

This wasn't helping him to understand why Dad had wanted the book so desperately. "Are there any other inscriptions connected with Hellicks in the book?"

"Why yes. Vivian mentions the inscriptions on the monolith at Periglis, although no one in living memory has ever seen it or them. It was destroyed in a great inundation centuries ago, although there are still some remnants of it if you know where to search."

Gray suddenly felt icy cold. Could this be the monolith he'd seen in his dream the night of the great storm? "What kind of inscriptions?"

"Difficult to explain them over the phone. But why this sudden interest?"

"Julie's grandfather was asking about them." Yet another lie, but Dad had expressly said he wasn't to tell anyone he was alive.

"Well, he didn't ask *me* about them," she said tetchily. "I suppose I could send him a photocopy."

"Could you send it to me? I could pass it on."

"If you think that's best. Now remember to label all my things, Gary, and stay around for the courier's arrival in the morning. Well, goodnight Gary. Let me know if you need anything else and I'll do my best to send it on. Marie's phone number is in the top drawer in the kitchen dresser."

His head spinning and his stomach complaining from lack of food, Gray went down to the kitchen, ate the contents of one of the tins of beans and fried himself the last two remaining eggs. He felt considerably better after that and although it was almost midnight he decided to parcel up his aunt's belongings just in case the courier arrived early next morning. Besides, he needed to stay awake as long as possible just in case Dad rang back.

CHAPTER 23

▼

Despite all his good intentions, Gray soon found his head nodding and he crept back upstairs, propped himself up on the bed, but with all the will in the world he was unable to stay awake. He slept fitfully at first, pursued by ghoulish dreams, but towards dawn fell into a heavy slumber.

When he awoke the sky was a pure washed blue with no sign of fog. He glanced at his watch and shot out of bed. It was gone nine and he was sure Julie's flight would have left by now. He'd been so convinced she'd call him.

At the first ring he nearly fell over himself to get to the phone in time.

"Hi Gray," it was Julie. She sounded dispirited. Her voice was so unlike her normal bouncy tone. "I'm in 'Departures' waiting for the nine-fifteen flight. I'm fed up at having to leave. Dead mean behaviour of Granps. He's changed so much since he got in with this SIPP gang. How'd you take it when he rang you?"

"I couldn't believe he'd do that to you."

"Yea, I was hopping mad. Still am. The plus side is I'll have no guilt now about coming back to visit you on Hellicks, but the down side is this wretched curfew business."

"It'll not last. Bet you it'll be over soon," said Gray, trying to convince himself as well as Julie.

"I'm just going to be out there as soon as it's over—with or without Mum. I'll find the money somehow. Sorry I couldn't convince Granps about investigating the tusk. They think what's happening is a whole lot bigger than they thought at first, some huge sort of source of power. If it's so big I can't understand why they can't locate it."

"Or perhaps it's not as huge as they think. Maybe the contents are, but not the container."

"Whee!" She gave a long whistling sound. "Yea! I see where you're at. I get your drift. I wonder if …" she was interrupted by the sound of an intercom. "Oh! Drat! They're calling us to switch off all mobiles and to watch the safety video. Got to go! Take …" there was a click and her voice ceased abruptly.

Gray pulled on his jeans and sweater. Better stop letting his thoughts run round in circles, better go now to do something to take his mind off things, feed the animals, collect some fresh eggs and dig up some potatoes. He rather fancied making potato fritters the way Charlotte used to make them. He'd watched her often enough to be sure he could make a go of it.

But first he'd better clear up the mess in the flat. Then he really ought to call on Jed and ask for some support. The way he kept being targeted by the Trevericks couldn't be allowed to go on and whoever was responsible for last night couldn't be left unpunished.

If only Dad would ring. Dad please, please ring back.

He crossed the yard to the flat and shoved the broken glass into a heap with his foot, swearing under his breath. Now he was going to have to board up yet another window. He glanced inside and in the clarity of the morning light noticed that although he'd been aware of the state of disorder last night, what he hadn't fully realised was that all the books from the bookshelves had been thrown onto the floor. Could it be that whoever the intruders were, they might have been looking for a book? Well, he thought, that ruled out the Trevericks.

But why a book? The idea was preposterous, it was crazy to think that. How could they possibly have known? He was just going to put the idea right out of his mind. As he shuffled through the pile on the floor in the wild hope that the Vivian book might still be there he noticed something odd. Where were Rob's science fiction books? Then it dawned on him as he searched. Every one of Rob's books on legends and magic had gone, completely disappeared.

Still puzzling and feeling rather sick, nonetheless he fed the animals and went off to the field to dig the vegetables. When he returned, laden with a sack of cabbages and potatoes and a basket of eggs, he saw a red haired young man wearing jeans and a T-shirt emblazoned with the words 'Island Couriers' standing by the farmhouse door. It was then he remembered his aunt's injunction to stay around first thing in the morning to await the arrival of the courier.

Gray placed his bounty on the doorstep and opened the door.

"Everything's parcelled up and ready. I'd just forgotten you were calling this morning," he said apologetically.

"Not surprising," said the young man. "I didn't think I'd get here anyway what with the barrage across the Sound between

Gugh and Porth Conger. I had to bring the boat round to Periglis. Don't know what's going on, do you? They said in Hugh Town, on Mary's, that there was something strange happening. Got to close both Hellicks' quays by noon, they said."

But Gray shook his head and shrugged his shoulders pretending he knew nothing.

"Oh! Miss Golighy sent me this fax and asked me to deliver it; said you'd know what it was all about." He handed Gray a folded sheet of paper. "Now if you can let me have those parcels I'll be off before my boat gets marooned."

Gray slipped the paper into his jeans' pocket and helped to load the courier's trolley with his aunt's parcels. He watched until the man had disappeared from sight and then pulled out the sheet of paper and unfolded it.

What he saw there made him gasp.

His aunt had written, 'According to Vivian these inscriptions were on the Periglis stone.'

Gray stared until the paper danced before his eyes.

He was looking at exactly the same markings as those on the tusk.

*   *   *   *

Something weird and unnerving in its outlandishness was happening. Gray thought he'd had a grasp of it when he was speaking to Julie but now he felt miles away from the real meaning. It was like trying to take hold of a jellyfish. There were clues but they didn't add up. There was the whole mystery of what Dad knew and why he wasn't communicating it. What or who was stopping him? If he'd known about the inscriptions in Vivian and if he knew what the connection was, why hadn't he told him? And what had he meant about the danger to the island? It didn't take a leap of imagination though to understand that Dad was clearly in danger himself and that he was afraid of his phone being tapped. But what was the connection between Dad, the symbols on the tusk and the Periglis stone?

His aunt had also copied a few verses the author, Vivian, had translated from the Icelandic, but if they were supposed to be a translation of the symbols it was not clear.

You knew we would come back,
flooding your fields, battering your walls,
howling revenge, cracking our whip in distant ice.
We waited, stalking, skulking, baiting,
Waiting for you to act, to heed the dark threat in the skies.
Like beguiled children you were asleep, you did not care until
you heard
Our knocking in your hearts; our payment overdue.

There was more, but it didn't particularly make sense to Gray. He was more interested in the markings. What really puzzled him was if the Periglis stone had been demolished centuries ago and no one knew about these markings except scholars like this Vivian chap, how did they come to be on the tusk? Did that mean the tusk itself was centuries old? And if the intruders did take the Vivian book, why would they do that? What could they possibly have known? And why remove all Rob's books about legends?

His head hurt with thinking and his stomach ached. He decided he'd better start making something to eat.

Making potato cakes was harder work than he'd imagined. He scraped his knuckles on the cheese grater making them bleed as he grated the raw potatoes into pulp. Then he dumped far too much flour into the gooey mess in the bowl and had to add more raw pulp so that he could mould the cakes into neat rounds. But after they'd been dropped into smoking hot fat and he'd watched them like a hawk to stop them burning, Gray felt a primitive sort of satisfaction like a hunter who'd bagged, and was now eating, his own quarry.

He sat down at the kitchen table munching away and listening to the news on the radio. An announcer was reading a statement about shipping hazards in the Atlantic and issuing a warning to all shipping in the area of the Western Isles and Bishop Rock. *It is not known whether the unusual signals and increased radiation is due to natural causes. Terrorist activity cannot be ruled out but so far there has been no evidence of any suspicious objects. Islanders in the vicinity have been warned that there could be a danger to fishing and animal life. There have been reported incidents of effects on animal behaviour but it is not thought to be having any undue effect on humans.*

Gray listened with a kind of growing fury. Well, something was certainly affecting human behaviour on St Hellicks. He was also convinced now that Dad and Rob had fallen into the hands of a group with violent intentions despite the flannelling on the radio. What was going to happen now?

There was a loud knock at the door. After last night Gray's first instinct was to ignore it. But when the knock was repeated and he heard a voice he recognised as Jed's calling his name, he changed his mind and went to answer it.

Jed stood there, his shirt sleeves rolled up to his elbows, his large hands clenching and unclenching, the movement at odds with his strong jutting chin and raw boned face. With him was Bob Stirling whose eyes were steely cold.

"I would have come over sooner," said Jed, "but the islanders had a meeting I had to attend. I don't hold with this harassment that's been going on, and for Tom's sake I'm prepared to stand by you. I have to abide by my own folk, but I reckon you've been badly treated."

"I don't agree Jed," said Bob. "We've never trusted you Edmonds but now you've stirred something that goes very deep and we want you out."

"*I've* stirred something deep?" Gray spluttered, beside himself with anger. "And who are *we* exactly? The ones who were chanting and swearing outside the house last night and who smashed the door to the flat? Or the Trevericks who threw the lighted petrol into the farm kitchen and drowned my aunt's cat?"

"Oh aye, now I was coming to that, about the cat I mean," said Bob. "And no, it's not just the Trevericks, it's the majority of us folk here who are against you, though not all of them are vandals. You've got their backs up. Like when you was seen practising that weird stuff with the seals. We've had centuries of contact with the sea and the stones on this island and no one comes here interfering with that."

"How am I supposed to have done that?" Gray said sharply.

"When things go wrong in a small place like this," interposed Jed, "where everybody knows everybody's business, it's easy to assume it's the ones who don't belong who're plotting against the rest."

"Now steady on Jed," said Bob. "Whose side are ye on?"

"But I'm not plotting anything against anybody, never have. I only wanted to be friendly, to join in."

"Ah," said Bob darkly. "Joining in, you calls it? Do you abide by our ways then? Share your produce and your catch or barter like the rest on us? Then there's the cat. Like you said, 'twas found drowned, dead as dead could be, and by some magic you bring it back to life, scaring folk out of their minds. Then we hear as how you conjures up the seals and talks to them. But worse, you bring a narwahl tusk that's cursed and marked with symbols. An' for sure that's what's at the back of why this island's being curfewed."

"I didn't bring it." Gray tried to stay calm. "It was washed up from the sea. Tom'd tell you if he was here."

"An' I wasn't going to mention that," said Bob. "But sod it! That was another member of your clan as drove Tom out. That damned aunt of yours."

Gray shook his head at the impossibility of reasoning with such accusations.

"Come, Bob, that doesn't warrant throwing petrol and smashing windows, now, does it?" said Jed, taking his arm, trying to breach Bob's fury.

"Anyways we're giving him chance to leave," said Bob, pushing Jed away. "That's better than some would have it and I wouldn't like to say what might happen to him if he don't."

"Come now! You promised. No threats," said Jed. "Let the lad leave and freely."

Bob turned to Jed. "Aye, but there's talk though of the legend."

"Not now," said Jed. "No need to talk of that."

"Nah!" said the other angrily. "There's folks here as believes in that legend. Molly Stokes tells that her grandfer told her that if ever the Perigilis stone was found again St Hellicks 'd drown just like the old Casseritides an' be lost forever under the waves."

"But the stone hasn't been found again," said Gray.

"No? But them symbols has," said Bob. "The same symbols as is on the tusk you brought to the island."

How did he know that? thought Gray. Then it dawned. They must have found Dad's copy of Vivian when they broke into the flat. "I keep telling you I didn't bring the tusk here and the symbols on the tusk aren't a curse. They're a protection." Gray bit his lip for he realised he'd said too much.

"So you do know all about it? An' it's right what the others are saying. You are the cause of everything that's affecting us right now, ain't you? You did bring the curse back to the island wi' this tusk o' yours. If I was you I'd clear out now before 'tis too late. The islanders are in a nasty mood I can tell you." Bob pushed his face up close to Gray's. "I'm warning you now for the last time. Clear out!" Then he stalked off muttering to himself.

"He's right lad. The islanders are not in a reasonable frame of mind right now. They're saying you're to blame for whatever it is that's causing the danger to the boats, and are the cause of their poor catches and their sick cattle, among other things. It mayn't make sense to you. But for generations we've suffered so much bad luck at sea, it's a way of life to believe in signs and portents; in Sculla, the goddess of the sea, and in our own St. Warna. It's in the blood."

Gray clapped his hand to his forehead. "And you Jed? Do you believe in those things?"

"I try to keep things in proportion, but there's no smoke without fire. I warned you before that you were behaving very odd. Then there's the question of the slashed wreath by Warna's well."

"I had nothing to do with that."

"Yet you were seen there around the time the damage was done."

Gray had always had his suspicions that his aunt in her fury over the loss of Co'burn had been responsible for the wreath's destruction but kept quiet. It was all too late now. The accusations were mounting up against him.

"If I were you I'd pack up something quick and get off in *Sea Rover* afore they blockade Periglis. It's only just coming up to midday and they promised to keep one quay open till then."

"Where do you suppose I'd go?"

"Go to Mary's, lad, then take the boat for the mainland, is my advice. Stay with your aunt till it blows over. Look," Jed's face softened. "I'll lend you the money for the fare."

"No need," said Gray, jutting out his chin proudly. "I've got money of my own, but I'm not leaving."

"The more fool you, then. I'll not be able to lift a finger to help you when they come for you. They weren't pretending, you know, about the legend. You might know of it?"

"No!"

"Then I'll tell you. Bob Stirling only talked about the first bit, about what the Periglis stone foretold about the coming of the floods," Jed 's voice took on an exaggeratedly dramatic tone, "of the heaving, twisting sea roaring up the cliffs hurling rocks and wrack. But he didn't say anything about the part where Sculla will be seen riding on the wild white foam pleading with her angry consort the god of the sea. And how the sea will crush the heart of us … unless …"

Into Gray's head came the verses that his aunt had sent with the symbols. The prophetic verses translated by Vivian from the ancient Icelandic:

"You knew we would come back.... howling revenge....
You did not care until you heard our knocking in your hearts:
our payment overdue. "

He was listening only to an inner voice, an inner knowing of what the ancient prophecy meant. The revenge ... the payment, was for slaughtering whales, polluting the seas, destroying marine life, for everything contributing to the widespread melting of glaciers, sea ice and destruction of polar creatures' habitats. It was nothing to do with the islanders' superstitious belief in magic.

"No!" he cried out, trying to push the nightmare away. But the look on Jed's face brought him back to the present.

"You said, unless ... Unless what?" Gray asked shivering.

"Unless ... a victim is sacrificed to the god of the sea."

"What! There're no such things as sea gods. I can't believe this is happening."

"It doesn't matter what you believe. The islanders have got to hold onto their beliefs, that's all they've got."

"What are they? Human beings or savages? God! This is the twenty-first century. You can't mean it?" Gray shook his head slowly as he looked directly into Jed's eyes, but the older man's face had become expressionless and he turned away saying, "Pack a bag now and go before it's too late."

CHAPTER 24

▼

After Jed had gone Gray drew the bolts on the door and stood for several minutes with his back against it. His heart was beating violently. Outside, the world was full of menace and an awful unknown. The islanders seemed to be suffering from a massive communal brainstorm. If only he could get a message through to Dad.

If he left now Dad would never know how to contact him again. But if he didn't leave? It didn't bear thinking about. He suddenly spurted into action, grabbed his haversack, stuffed it with the remains of the potato cakes and the last tin of coke, dashed upstairs and rolled a clean t-shirt, his toothbrush and toiletries into a towel. He'd have to ring Aunt Aleyne from St Mary's; there wasn't time now.

He passed no-one as he bounded down to the old quay and waded across to the dinghy. It was then he noticed an official looking craft coming into the bay. Gray rowed over to *Sea Rover*, left the dinghy at anchor, and climbed aboard.

The strange craft was sailing in closer. A man on deck dressed in uniform hailed him with, "Where do you think you're going?" But Gray ignored him and started up the engine. There was the sound of a loud crack across *Sea Rover's* bows and Gray realised with a shock that he'd been fired at. What was this? Was everyone at war with him?

"You won't get a second warning," the officer called as the craft came alongside. "I asked you where you think you're going? Everyone's been told. No shipping out of here and no shipping in, for the next twenty-four hours."

"But it's an emergency," said Gray, keeping the engine running.

"What kind of emergency?"

Gray could just picture the man's face if he told him what was happening on Hellicks.

"It's personal ... My dad ..." he began, trying to stop the shutter coming down in his mind blanking out his thoughts.

"Is he ill? Is it a medical emergency?"

"Uh!" Gray stuttered

"All medical emergencies will be dealt with by helicopter. No boats leave this quay. That's an order. Now get back home boy or you'll be under arrest."

The engine cut out and Gray stared uncomprehendingly at the man in the uniform

"I'm sorry," said the man. "Rules are rules. Go home—don't cause trouble."

Trouble! Gray thought. He was in trouble up to his neck.

The day felt heavy and airless. There was a distant flash of light over the sea followed by a clap of thunder.

"Storm coming," said the man. "Get going boy, while you can."

Reluctantly Gray pulled in the mooring ropes and climbed back into the dinghy. He rowed back to land like a condemned prisoner, stumbled onto the shore and lay there stunned, motionless, letting the big drops of rain fall unheeded on his face, neck and bare head.

At last he stood up, defeated and soaking, and made his way through the fields back to the farm. He barricaded the door by pulling the settee against it and piling a chest of drawers on top of that. He sat, unable to think, waiting for the attack. But none came.

The clouds opened and water poured down in floods. The yard was adrift with streaming muddy rivulets within minutes. It was as if sluice gates had opened and the prophecy was about to be fulfilled. The rain continued into the late afternoon. Outside, flowerpots, buckets and old sacking floated in the rising waters.

Towards evening the rain stopped. Gray, becoming increasingly anxious, toyed with the idea of ringing James to ask for help, but knew it was too late. What could he do? And why would he believe Gray was beleaguered in his own house waiting to be sacrificed to the god of the sea? Nothing James had ever done or said led Gray to believe he would give credence to such a monstrous idea. Perhaps it was a monstrous idea, some sort of joke. After all, no one had actually named him the chosen victim. Yet he could not forget the haggard expression on Jed's face nor the tone of his voice as he urged him to leave.

In his heart he knew the Trevericks were behind this. It was no joke. They were never going to leave him alone. He'd been outlawed from the start, had never stood a chance and this was the finale.

Then he thought of Julie and he reproached himself for giving in so easily. He could hear her challenging him. Was he really such a wimp? As he rallied he began to review the situation more rationally. The islanders had got it all wrong. If Vivian's verses were a translation of the symbols which appeared on the Periglis stone and again on the tusk, the *'dark threat in the skies'* could not mean flooding by sea. In fact they didn't seem to have got anything right. He remembered his vivid dream in which the Old Man of Gugh spoke to him saying, "The waters will not come again, not ever again." At the time the words hadn't meant anything to Gray. But now it all fitted. Yet over the centuries the legends must have become distorted.

The islanders were behaving like superstitious savages. But they were humans too and he couldn't believe they intended his death just to satisfy an outdated myth. That was too grotesque. They just wanted to frighten him to make him pay for the curfew which they mistakenly held him responsible for. He was sure he could reason with them, appeal to them.

Then he heard the squelching sound as of many boots treading water and the muttering of voices … Then that awful, mindless chanting began again. It swelled and faded, swelled and faded, as if directed by a nameless authority. But above the cacophony he felt that familiar sickening vibration.

Gray froze on the spot as the chanting suddenly ceased and a voice he didn't recognise called out "One, Two, Three … Heave." The door juddered and the chest of drawers fell off the settee with a loud clatter but the makeshift barricade held.

Gray's survival instincts sent him leaping up the stairs three at a time, his haversack clutched in his hands. From the attic window he looked down on a sea of heads. At a quick calculation he reckoned there must be upwards of thirty. In the midst he thought he recognised Rod Treverick's head. He appeared to be urging the others on. The evil little hunched up Agnes by his side was carrying the cursed tusk.

The massed menace charged again. The door couldn't hold out much longer.

The symbols! They had helped him before. He drew them in the air with a trembling hand and as he did his mind cleared and a plan began to form. There was no back exit from the farm but years ago he and Rob had once abseiled from the landing into the lane behind. Sure enough the hook they'd used was still there deeply lodged into the sill. The rope would surely be there too, somewhere in the attic. He pushed books and boxes out of the way feverishly searching when he heard the first mighty splintering of the door and a raucous shout. At last he found the rope coiled up in a corner under a pile of old clothes. He must hurry. Would the hook still hold? He must be twice the weight since those early days. Fortunately the rope still bore its original slipknot. He drew it over the hook, threw his haversack down so that it landed softly on the grass verge and slid down gingerly. The hook held until he was only feet from the ground then it snapped sending him flying, but he was safe. He jerked the rope free and wrapping it round his waist headed for the bay. Once they'd broken into the house it wouldn't be long before they'd start to search. They knew the places to look, places that had been used for centuries to hide contraband and other illegal goods.

But his plan was to cross over to Burnt Island where the tusk had first been found. He knew deep clefts in the rocks where a man could lie hidden for days. The islanders had always held the tiny island in dread. There was a kind of superstitious fear that the place was haunted so perhaps they wouldn't follow him there and he'd be safe. If his luck held the tide would soon cover his tracks. He prayed the causeway was not yet covered by the incoming tide so that he could cross over. It was already rushing in as Gray slithered and slid over rocks and pebbles wet with wrack while the noise of seagulls and the crashing waves bore in on him.

At last he was beyond reach of the tide. He could hear it sucking in and out of the strange brown and black boulders that gave the place its name. The whole island looked as though it had survived a massive fire. No vegetation grew here, not even the common samphire. He could hole up here until the barrage was removed. At worst he could swim the channel between the island and Butterman's Point on Annet which must be no more than half a kilometre away. It was a desperate and last ditch plan as the seas at this time of year were arctic cold and there were hidden razor sharp reefs that could rip his limbs to shreds and that was not counting the notorious currents between the two islands that could tow him under.

Gray looked down into the dark space called Devils' Chasm. Although he knew every stone and rock on Burnt Island he had never dared to drop down into this cleft. He was glad he'd had the foresight to bring the rope and found he could hook the slipknot over a protruding jagged edge and let himself down into the murky depths. Feeling with his feet he realised he had reached the corner of a large crack in the rock. He wedged his right foot in by twisting it on one side. His ankle throbbed as the foot twisted but he was able to swing the other foot over and get a hold on the side of the crack. Tentatively he explored the surfaces of rock and found he could heave and scrape his way up into a kind of hollow chamber.

As he got used to the dark he could make out a ledge deep enough for him to lie down full length. It was dark and eerie. This part of the island had been his private sanctuary ever since he was old enough to cross the causeway and he had never been afraid of being alone here. But this time it was different. He was planning to stay throughout the night.

He pulled the rolled up towel out of his bag for a pillow, rationed himself by eating only one of the potato cakes and drinking half the can of coke and tried to sleep but was prevented by drops of moisture dripping constantly from the roof of the chamber, accompanied by strange gurgling sounds and the slitherings of small squelchy creatures. There was a stale dank smell and as the atmosphere was incredibly close and airless he found it difficult to breathe.

He tried to argue with himself that they would grow tired of looking for him and would come to their senses once the curfew was lifted and they could go back to their everyday lives. If only he could last out until then. Only the rest of the night and the next morning to go. But then the remembrance of the passionate angry voices in the yard and the strange hold the tusk seemed to have over everyone, made him doubt his reasoning.

The mysterious gurgling noise grew louder and a feeling of deep loneliness and horror at the weirdness of it all set him trembling.

The islanders had never welcomed him before but they'd never hated him enough to want his death. It was the coming of the narwhal tusk that had changed them. The spell would not be broken while the tusk remained on the island.

Shivers ran up and down his spine. He was out of control. A sick feeling of fear and rage swept over him. Although he was exhausted he could not let go and relax into sleep. Lying there in the darkness he could not even summon up the energy to draw on the power of the symbols. On the sea, in *Sea Rover*, it had been different. Here in almost pitch darkness with night coming on he felt out of touch with everything, most of all with so-called magical power. It was that which had been the cause all this trouble in the first place. His faith abandoned him. The despair of the Devil's Chasm, the tales of centuries of drownings and wandering shipwrecked ghosts gripped him as he sank deep into a nightmare of slimy sea monsters breathing, sucking and slithering over him.

CHAPTER 25

▼

Gray awoke from the nightmare coughing, almost choking, unable to remember where he was. He could smell smoke and became aware of it seething down the narrow neck of the cleft. He sat up, banging his head on the roof of the chamber, alert and afraid. He slid out feet first, trying to stifle the noise of his coughing as the smoke filtered down. He heaved himself up on the rope using his knees and feet to lever himself up until he could finally take hold of a boulder at the mouth of the crevice and pull himself up and out. He choked again as a blanket of smoke engulfed him. He could hear muffled voices and saw flames that seemed to be leaping through the smoke and knew he was trapped.

They were going to smoke him out or burn him alive. He remembered the desperate plan he'd formed as a last resort. He was going to have to swim for it. The rule was no shipping out or in but that didn't apply to swimmers.

A wind was getting up, whipping the smoke and flames, bringing them ever closer but also wafting a weird ululating sound that seemed to be coming from the other side of the bay. Gray stumbled over stones and boulders until he reached a vantage point at the tip of the island overlooking the long arm of St. Hellicks that jutted out to sea. What he saw made him gasp in disbelief. A group of islanders, he was unable to identify them at this distance, were chanting and dancing in circle at the base of the huge bear shaped rock, known as Mount Point. He was sure he could make out the tusk being carried aloft by a figure in the centre of the circle. They were clearly celebrating his plight and glorying in the blazing incandescence that was now Burnt Island. The flames would be visible for miles and would attract the coast guard. But by the time they arrived it would be too late.

With the fire roaring at his back he had two choices, death by fire or water. Even if he managed to cross the Sound between this and Annett, the next island, there was the danger of being ripped apart by the razor like reefs surrounding Annett.

If only he could call his friends the seals. He needed their knowledge. They were the only creatures that could help him now. They alone knew the big flat rocks where one could heave oneself safely out of the churning sea. But how would they hear at this distance?

He called without expecting that there would be time enough for them to reach him even if they heard. He called again but the wind was whipping the smoke higher and forcing the sound back down his throat. His heart raced in fear. Then in the next instant he felt the connection, smelt their smell in the air. He knew they had heard him. They would come, surely they would come.

There was a tremulous sound and he saw the round black head of a seal bobbing in the water. Soon the sea was alive with their sleek heads, their muzzles raised, waiting, as if for a signal. The signal came; a deep grunting sound from the leading bull.

It was echoed by dozens more swimming in to answer the call. It seemed to Gray that the sea boiled with thousands of sea creatures coming to his rescue.

On the opposite shore the dancers had halted their chanting and were standing stock still in utter amazement. One uttered a shriek and ran down to the shore and then they all followed rushing headlong down to the edge of the sea to witness the incredible arrival of so many sea creatures. They watched with growing dismay and superstitious fear as seals and porpoises began to slowly straddle the low-lying rocks. And when it looked as though the rescue of their victim was imminent they let out an angry roar and Gray saw one of them cast the tusk into the sea as if to rid themselves of the cursed legend.

Lost. Oh! Lost ... his tusk now lost forever.

More than anything Gray wanted to believe in the magic of the symbols. Even if the tusk was lost he still had the power to evoke their help. They had always been his protection and guide. Why was he hesitating now? He'd dismissed them in the darkness of his long night in Devil's Chasm. He had lost faith in them. Yet he hadn't found them. They had found him. He was meant to use the symbols. He was going to die anyway now. Even with the help of the seals, in such arctic cold waters there was little hope of him crossing Smith Sound alive.

The heat of the flames was burning the back of his neck. But his fingers tingled with an unmistakable vibration. There was no mistake. The symbols were calling him, guiding him.

Concentrate, just concentrate. Believe, trust as you've never trusted before.

This was not the moment to hesitate. He let all caution go and raising his arms in the air drew the symbols, remembering them clearly and accurately. He drew them over and over again. Vividly, passionately.

He was aware of a massive jolting through the soles of his feet, a loud booming sound reverberating across the water. Gray watched open mouthed as the vast bear shaped rock shuddered. There was a screeching yell from the dancers as the rock appeared to move imperceptibly and then it slowly rolled over. Like a great lumbering beast it bore down in heavy pounding progression, taking boulders, huge ferns, in its relentless path down to the sea, knocking everything aside like skittle pins.

With his friends the seals clustered round nudging him and grunting Gray knew there was no time to lose. He stripped quickly and knotted his hair back. If entering the dark hole of Devil's Chasm had been a challenge, this was worse. His years of swimming in the icy Atlantic waters had not prepared him for the pain that surged through him as his body hit the water. His whole body felt as though it was on fire and the pain was excruciating. The seals were swimming in formation beside him occasionally diving beneath the surface but remaining always as guides directing him on, on towards Annett.

Then the cramps began and he turned over on his back with his legs doubled up trying to keep afloat by using backstroke. As he flipped over he could see that the whole island was ablaze, the sky was black and a heavy smoke pall was drifting over the sea.

> *Must keep going.*
> *Must keep going.*
> *Show me where to land safely.*

A large bull seal grunted and nudged him pushing him, gently, urging him forward.

His body was losing all sensation, his mind unaware of direction and yet there just beyond reach the tusk was floating out to sea. With one last huge burst of energy he reached out and grasped it, edging his fingers round the knobbly surface. It was his at last, it was …

There was another sound above the booming of the waves— a deep yet distant whirring and buzzing as though the whole ocean was churning up. He knew he recognised the sound from somewhere but the cramp was blacking out his mind. He struck out with his arms.

Got to get to shore.
Got to get to shore.

Then there were rocks grazing the back of his hands, tearing the flesh. He was a shivering mass of jelly. The whirring sound was closing in, closer, closer. A huge dark shape blotted out his sight. This was the terror of the end, '*the dark threat from the skies*'. He gave in and slipped down the black slope of death.

*   *   *   *

Gray opened his eyes and looked up at a white coat, a dangling stethoscope, another white coat. Anxious, strange faces.

He groaned. His chest hurt, his hands were burning.

"You're a lucky fellow," said one of the white coats. "Your body temperature had fallen to 34°C by the time the helicopter got to you. Most people would have drowned within minutes of being in such intense cold. No need to ask what you were doing."

There was a polite cough.

"Oh, there's someone to see you."

Dad, oh, Dad!

But it wasn't Dad.

"How are ye lad?

Instead he saw Tom staring down at him, his kind old eyes brimming with tears and there was Charlotte next to him.

"We should never 'ave left ye, we should never. And then when we found yer aunt 'ad gone away ..." Tom choked.

"How she could 'ave done that beats me," said Charlotte.

"What were ye thinking of trying to swim across Smith Sound?" asked Tom. "Strong as ye are ye'd never 'ave made it. The coast guards say they saw the strangest thing they'd ever seen. An 'alf drowned lad slung across the back of a great bull seal accompanied by a whole school of 'em. They swore that if they 'adn't seen it with their own eyes they would never 'ave believed it."

Gray blinked and shook his head slowly as understanding swam into his mind. But what about the fire?

"But the fire ...?" He croaked hoarsely

Tom leaned over and whispered. "It was the Trevericks, lad. Tried to smoke ye out. An' they would have succeeded in doing worse if it hadn't been for Jed. They're banged up now the lot o' them."

"The rock ... at Mount Point?"

"Aye, that. No one knows what caused it. An earth tremor it was, like we've never seen on Hellicks before."

"No one hurt?"

"Badly shaken I would say but none hurt."

"How did you come to find out?"

"Jed Rowe. He wouldn't 'ave let 'em 'arm ye. 'E's a good man is Jed. 'E rang us at Catherine's, our daughter's 'ouse, last night. We came over by the first flight. I knew where ye'd be 'iding better than any of 'em but it was Jed called the 'elicopter."

"But the island, the fire? How did they …?"

"'Tis all over now, don't ye fret. Wasna' any of 'em save the Trevericks as started it."

"They hate me … all the islanders hate me. I can't go back there."

"No lad … no! It wasna' ye that was the cause."

Gray looked at him dumbly and had a fleeting vision of the seals. He was hearing the message they had given him that night in Warna's bay. And he knew that they were right, there was nowhere else in the world where he belonged. But he was still not sure he could return.

"I tell ye, it was something else. I don't rightly understand it but they'll explain it to ye. They'll explain what caused it. Don't say as ye can't go back till ye've heard."

Gray nodded, unsure who 'they' were.

"An there's more, if ye can take it lad."

Gray saw Charlotte touch Tom's hand. "No, not now Tom. Let the lad rest."

"No, it's happy news Charlotte an' my 'eart's bursting to tell. 'E 'as to know."

Know what?

"Ye Dad and Rob's alive an' well. They're alive lad," and Tom's face shone through his tears.

"It's alright Tom … I know," whispered Gray ever so quietly.

But Tom went on as though he hadn't heard. "The *Minerva* was found grounded in a cove off the mainland. Mystery was, there weren't any survivors, 'cos ye Dad and Rob had been nabbed by a group as was targeting Hellicks. And of course,"

Tom paused to take a breath, "this gang didn't want 'em going back to the island and spilling on 'em, did they, eh lad?"

"Oh, get on with it Tom," said Charlotte.

"The police was keeping quiet like until they got the gang that captured 'em. It was a group calls themselves ..." He turned to Charlotte, "What was it, the name, we was told?"

Charlotte shook her head. It was all clearly beyond her.

"Well, never mind the name, they was charging objects with 'igh electrical frequencies and targeting small communities like Hellicks. Some sort of terrible experiment of sending out signals to the brain that couldn't be 'eard by the 'uman ear but was acting on folk's behaviour making them do all sorts of terrible things. Controlling them like. And what's more, they was using objects like that tusk of yours with its old writing on so that folks'd believe they'd come special like. So that it all tied in with their beliefs. That was it, wasn't it Charlotte? Never knew they could do such things."

"No," said Charlotte. "Ye never knows what things they can do to control us these days."

Gray's mind was racing ahead. So why hadn't he been affected? He'd had proof enough of the amazing power of the symbols. Was it possible that their ancient power was stronger than modern technology? Were they a sort of protection, as he'd always believed?

"It didn't act only on human behaviour, Tom. Remember my aunt's cat?"

"I do that! Dratted animal! So, that's what made it go off like a mad thing."

"I expect so. You see, I found out most of it because Dad managed to phone me. But only the once. I never heard again but I put two and two together."

"Oh! Well now. That gang's been banged up too an' there's going to be a lot o' questions to answer over this lot. But wait till I tell ye more …" Tom beamed. "The best of it is, Jed's 'ere, just waiting till I give ye the good news," his smile broadened. "Then we're off to meet ye Dad and Rob at the airport. I'll just go and get 'im."

When Jed came in he was carrying a familiar object whose tip he placed in Gray's bandaged hands, laying the whole tusk across the bed.

"It's rightly yours now. And it'll cause no more trouble," said Jed with a smile. "The science boffins have dismantled it and it's as innocent as the day it sat on the end of a narwhal's nose."

"We'll all be off now. Get some rest to be ready for when ye Dad comes," said Charlotte, brushing his cheek with her lips. "Ye're going to need it. Ye'll have a lot to catch up on."

Alone once more, Gray at last gave way to his feelings. All the pent up agony of loss long held inside, and the terrifying remembrance of how fragile human minds could be so monstrously twisted, swept over him. He wept for the destruction of the precious place that was his own private contact with the rocks and the sea, now tarnished by the memory of bitter hatred and superstition.

He only partly believed in Tom's interpretation of what had been the cause. The way the tusk had been misused and manipulated was only one answer. The answer that the scientists were happy to give. But Gray knew better. He knew the real secret of the tusk and the magic that lay within the ancient symbols.

In his heart he felt it was too easy to dismiss the mystery of it all, the dreams, the prophecies, the strange magic that had been at work. That magic was part of St Hellicks and would always remain, defying any explanation. Yet he wondered if even with

Dad's, and Rob's help, he would ever recapture his joy in the island.

But then there was Julie. As soon as she knew what had happened she would, in her own words, 'be over like a shot'. There'd be no stopping her. She of all people would believe the truth about the tusk just as she believed in him.

At that moment a nurse came in to give him his medication.

"Oh! Bye the way," she said, handing him a glass of water. "There was a phone message left at reception by a Miss Julie something or other. She's heard about your accident and is coming over to stay. I think that's what she said."

Gray smiled. News travelled fast on these islands.

He felt a glow of happiness, and stronger and wiser than he had ever been. He let his bandaged hands slide over the tusk as it lay beside him and once again drew the ancient Icelandic symbols in the air. The message seemed clear. As long as we lived in harmony with each other, respecting each others' differences, not trying to change another's way of life, and giving the same respect to nature, '*the waters would never come again*'.

A sense of completion and peace entered the room.

The Narwhal tusk was at rest.

978-0-595-48177-4
0-595-48177-9

Printed in the United Kingdom
by Lightning Source UK Ltd.
129482UK00001B/121/A